THE GIRL HE TOOK

(A Paige King Mystery—Book Three)

BLAKE PIERCE

Blake Pierce

Blake Pierce is the USA Today bestselling author of the RILEY PAGE mystery series, which includes seventeen books. Blake Pierce is also the author of the MACKENZIE WHITE mystery series, comprising fourteen books; of the AVERY BLACK mystery series, comprising six books; of the KERI LOCKE mystery series, comprising five books; of the MAKING OF RILEY PAIGE mystery series, comprising six books; of the KATE WISE mystery series, comprising seven books; of the CHLOE FINE psychological suspense mystery, comprising six books; of the JESSE HUNT psychological suspense thriller series, comprising twenty four books; of the AU PAIR psychological suspense thriller series, comprising three books; of the ZOE PRIME mystery series, comprising six books; of the ADELE SHARP mystery series, comprising fifteen books, of the EUROPEAN VOYAGE cozy mystery series, comprising four books; of the new LAURA FROST FBI suspense thriller, comprising nine books (and counting); of the new ELLA DARK FBI suspense thriller, comprising eleven books (and counting); of the A YEAR IN EUROPE cozy mystery series, comprising nine books, of the AVA GOLD mystery series, comprising six books (and counting); of the RACHEL GIFT mystery series, comprising eight books (and counting); of the VALERIE LAW mystery series, comprising nine books (and counting); of the PAIGE KING mystery series, comprising six books (and counting); of the MAY MOORE mystery series, comprising six books (and counting); and the CORA SHIELDS mystery series, comprising three books (and counting).

An avid reader and lifelong fan of the mystery and thriller genres, Blake loves to hear from you, so please feel free to visit www.blakepierceauthor.com to learn more and stay in touch.

ISBN: 978-1-0943-7729-2

BOOKS BY BLAKE PIERCE

CORA SHIELDS MYSTERY SERIES
UNDONE (Book #1)
UNWANTED (Book #2)
UNHINGED (Book #3)

MAY MOORE SUSPENSE THRILLER
NEVER RUN (Book #1)
NEVER TELL (Book #2)
NEVER LIVE (Book #3)
NEVER HIDE (Book #4)
NEVER FORGIVE (Book #5)
NEVER AGAIN (Book #6)

PAIGE KING MYSTERY SERIES
THE GIRL HE PINED (Book #1)
THE GIRL HE CHOSE (Book #2)
THE GIRL HE TOOK (Book #3)
THE GIRL HE WISHED (Book #4)
THE GIRL HE CROWNED (Book #5)
THE GIRL HE WATCHED (Book #6)

VALERIE LAW MYSTERY SERIES
NO MERCY (Book #1)
NO PITY (Book #2)
NO FEAR (Book #3)
NO SLEEP (Book #4)
NO QUARTER (Book #5)
NO CHANCE (Book #6)
NO REFUGE (Book #7)
NO GRACE (Book #8)
NO ESCAPE (Book #9)

RACHEL GIFT MYSTERY SERIES

HER LAST WISH (Book #1)
HER LAST CHANCE (Book #2)
HER LAST HOPE (Book #3)
HER LAST FEAR (Book #4)
HER LAST CHOICE (Book #5)
HER LAST BREATH (Book #6)
HER LAST MISTAKE (Book #7)
HER LAST DESIRE (Book #8)

AVA GOLD MYSTERY SERIES
CITY OF PREY (Book #1)
CITY OF FEAR (Book #2)
CITY OF BONES (Book #3)
CITY OF GHOSTS (Book #4)
CITY OF DEATH (Book #5)
CITY OF VICE (Book #6)

A YEAR IN EUROPE
A MURDER IN PARIS (Book #1)
DEATH IN FLORENCE (Book #2)
VENGEANCE IN VIENNA (Book #3)
A FATALITY IN SPAIN (Book #4)

ELLA DARK FBI SUSPENSE THRILLER
GIRL, ALONE (Book #1)
GIRL, TAKEN (Book #2)
GIRL, HUNTED (Book #3)
GIRL, SILENCED (Book #4)
GIRL, VANISHED (Book 5)
GIRL ERASED (Book #6)
GIRL, FORSAKEN (Book #7)
GIRL, TRAPPED (Book #8)
GIRL, EXPENDABLE (Book #9)
GIRL, ESCAPED (Book #10)
GIRL, HIS (Book #11)

LAURA FROST FBI SUSPENSE THRILLER
ALREADY GONE (Book #1)
ALREADY SEEN (Book #2)

ALREADY TRAPPED (Book #3)
ALREADY MISSING (Book #4)
ALREADY DEAD (Book #5)
ALREADY TAKEN (Book #6)
ALREADY CHOSEN (Book #7)
ALREADY LOST (Book #8)
ALREADY HIS (Book #9)

EUROPEAN VOYAGE COZY MYSTERY SERIES
MURDER (AND BAKLAVA) (Book #1)
DEATH (AND APPLE STRUDEL) (Book #2)
CRIME (AND LAGER) (Book #3)
MISFORTUNE (AND GOUDA) (Book #4)
CALAMITY (AND A DANISH) (Book #5)
MAYHEM (AND HERRING) (Book #6)

ADELE SHARP MYSTERY SERIES
LEFT TO DIE (Book #1)
LEFT TO RUN (Book #2)
LEFT TO HIDE (Book #3)
LEFT TO KILL (Book #4)
LEFT TO MURDER (Book #5)
LEFT TO ENVY (Book #6)
LEFT TO LAPSE (Book #7)
LEFT TO VANISH (Book #8)
LEFT TO HUNT (Book #9)
LEFT TO FEAR (Book #10)
LEFT TO PREY (Book #11)
LEFT TO LURE (Book #12)
LEFT TO CRAVE (Book #13)
LEFT TO LOATHE (Book #14)
LEFT TO HARM (Book #15)

THE AU PAIR SERIES
ALMOST GONE (Book#1)
ALMOST LOST (Book #2)
ALMOST DEAD (Book #3)

ZOE PRIME MYSTERY SERIES

FACE OF DEATH (Book#1)
FACE OF MURDER (Book #2)
FACE OF FEAR (Book #3)
FACE OF MADNESS (Book #4)
FACE OF FURY (Book #5)
FACE OF DARKNESS (Book #6)

A JESSIE HUNT PSYCHOLOGICAL SUSPENSE SERIES
THE PERFECT WIFE (Book #1)
THE PERFECT BLOCK (Book #2)
THE PERFECT HOUSE (Book #3)
THE PERFECT SMILE (Book #4)
THE PERFECT LIE (Book #5)
THE PERFECT LOOK (Book #6)
THE PERFECT AFFAIR (Book #7)
THE PERFECT ALIBI (Book #8)
THE PERFECT NEIGHBOR (Book #9)
THE PERFECT DISGUISE (Book #10)
THE PERFECT SECRET (Book #11)
THE PERFECT FAÇADE (Book #12)
THE PERFECT IMPRESSION (Book #13)
THE PERFECT DECEIT (Book #14)
THE PERFECT MISTRESS (Book #15)
THE PERFECT IMAGE (Book #16)
THE PERFECT VEIL (Book #17)
THE PERFECT INDISCRETION (Book #18)
THE PERFECT RUMOR (Book #19)
THE PERFECT COUPLE (Book #20)
THE PERFECT MURDER (Book #21)
THE PERFECT HUSBAND (Book #22)
THE PERFECT SCANDAL (Book #23)
THE PERFECT MASK (Book #24)

CHLOE FINE PSYCHOLOGICAL SUSPENSE SERIES
NEXT DOOR (Book #1)
A NEIGHBOR'S LIE (Book #2)
CUL DE SAC (Book #3)
SILENT NEIGHBOR (Book #4)
HOMECOMING (Book #5)

TINTED WINDOWS (Book #6)

KATE WISE MYSTERY SERIES
IF SHE KNEW (Book #1)
IF SHE SAW (Book #2)
IF SHE RAN (Book #3)
IF SHE HID (Book #4)
IF SHE FLED (Book #5)
IF SHE FEARED (Book #6)
IF SHE HEARD (Book #7)

THE MAKING OF RILEY PAIGE SERIES
WATCHING (Book #1)
WAITING (Book #2)
LURING (Book #3)
TAKING (Book #4)
STALKING (Book #5)
KILLING (Book #6)

RILEY PAIGE MYSTERY SERIES
ONCE GONE (Book #1)
ONCE TAKEN (Book #2)
ONCE CRAVED (Book #3)
ONCE LURED (Book #4)
ONCE HUNTED (Book #5)
ONCE PINED (Book #6)
ONCE FORSAKEN (Book #7)
ONCE COLD (Book #8)
ONCE STALKED (Book #9)
ONCE LOST (Book #10)
ONCE BURIED (Book #11)
ONCE BOUND (Book #12)
ONCE TRAPPED (Book #13)
ONCE DORMANT (Book #14)
ONCE SHUNNED (Book #15)
ONCE MISSED (Book #16)
ONCE CHOSEN (Book #17)

MACKENZIE WHITE MYSTERY SERIES

BEFORE HE KILLS (Book #1)
BEFORE HE SEES (Book #2)
BEFORE HE COVETS (Book #3)
BEFORE HE TAKES (Book #4)
BEFORE HE NEEDS (Book #5)
BEFORE HE FEELS (Book #6)
BEFORE HE SINS (Book #7)
BEFORE HE HUNTS (Book #8)
BEFORE HE PREYS (Book #9)
BEFORE HE LONGS (Book #10)
BEFORE HE LAPSES (Book #11)
BEFORE HE ENVIES (Book #12)
BEFORE HE STALKS (Book #13)
BEFORE HE HARMS (Book #14)

AVERY BLACK MYSTERY SERIES
CAUSE TO KILL (Book #1)
CAUSE TO RUN (Book #2)
CAUSE TO HIDE (Book #3)
CAUSE TO FEAR (Book #4)
CAUSE TO SAVE (Book #5)
CAUSE TO DREAD (Book #6)

KERI LOCKE MYSTERY SERIES
A TRACE OF DEATH (Book #1)
A TRACE OF MURDER (Book #2)
A TRACE OF VICE (Book #3)
A TRACE OF CRIME (Book #4)
A TRACE OF HOPE (Book #5)

CHAPTER ONE

Clarissa was a long way from comfortable when she arrived for the audition at the old theater, and not just because of the dress she decided would show off her figure to best effect in front of the director.

It was more to do with how quiet the theater was. Here in Vegas, the assumption was that everything that mattered was open 24-7, constantly glowing with neon lighting and as loud as possible to grab attention from all the other venues around; but the theater was silent and dark now. It was slightly dilapidated, not even on the main strip. It was the kind of place that Clarissa's instincts said she ought to just walk away from.

"Stop it," Clarissa told herself, in her sternest tone. She knew that was just nerves. She always got them before an audition, always felt like she should just run away. Even the auditions she made it into, those nerves came through. It was why it was taking so long to break through here, in spite of Las Vegas being one of the performance capitals of the world.

She had to embrace the nerves this time, use them to charge her performance and make it better. It didn't matter if the script she'd been sent wasn't good, or just a bit narration part in some magic show, or if the venue was small, or even that she was out there in the middle of the night for an audition.

What mattered was that, if she got this, then it was a part in a professional production, in Las Vegas. She could say that she'd been in a show, and that would make it easier to get parts in *other* shows. Slowly, Clarissa would build herself up, her name would get hot, and eventually…

Eventually it would be her name up on a billboard, drawing people into a show, in one of the big casinos or theaters. She would be the one making the big bucks as a star here. And if, for the moment, Clarissa could also make enough money from this show to actually pay her rent on time this month, that would be great too.

For all those reasons, Clarissa made her way around to the stage door, where the email asking her to the audition had told her to come. She checked her appearance carefully in a makeup mirror, wanting to make sure that she was perfect, primping her dark hair, applying one last layer of eyeshadow around her dark eyes, adjusting her deep blue dress.

She took a breath and then headed inside. The door was propped open by a brick, and Clarissa must have knocked it as she went through, because it slammed behind her, locked tight. The place was eerily quiet. Clarissa had been expecting someone to meet her at the door, but there was no one there. The only sign of life at all in the theater was that there were lights on, rows of them seeming to lead the way through it.

When they led up to the stage, Clarissa started to relax just a little. She was here to perform, after all.

"Hello?" Clarissa called out. "My name is Clarissa Bale. I'm here for the audition?"

She couldn't help a note of uncertainty in her voice. It wasn't just the usual audition nerves now. It was the strangeness of this whole situation. There should have been other girls there, reading for the part. There should have been *someone* there.

Her nervousness wasn't helped when music started playing out of nowhere, spotlights suddenly shining down on the stage, moving in arcs.

"Read your part," a voice said, coming out of one of the speakers.

In a way, that instruction was almost comforting, because at least it meant that someone was there. Clarissa had memorized her lines, of course. She wanted to be off book for the audition to show that she was a professional. Not that the part was that complex: a simple piece of narration.

"Chung Ling Soo, real name William Ellsworth Robinson, was one of the most famous magicians of the nineteenth and early twentieth centuries. Using his adopted persona to claim access to mysterious secrets, he told the world that he could catch bullets in his teeth. He kept going with his trick until a tragic misfire claimed his life in 1918."

Clarissa paused for emphasis, taking the opportunity to show that she could add more drama to the part. This might be a small narration gig, but Clarissa was going to fight hard for it.

"Since his death, the bullet catch has claimed the lives of more magicians than any other effect. Tonight, the greatest of those dead has risen again for your entertainment!"

The speakers poured out canned applause, presumably to give Clarissa a sense of what it would be like when a real audience was in there. It was one note of creepiness too much for Clarissa.

"Look," she called out. "What is all this? I came here for an audition, not for… whatever this is!"

There was no answer. Clarissa had enough. She turned to leave the stage, determined to find some other way out of there.

A figure moved onto the stage as she did so, wrapped from head to foot in bandages like a mummy. He was wearing a long leather coat and a fedora hat, the combination strange and incongruous.

He was carrying a large box with the word "bullets" scrawled on the front in red ink that would presumably be visible from back in the audience. Clarissa hesitated as the figure lurched towards her almost comically, playing the part of the risen dead almost perfectly. A part of her still wondered if this was all part of the same act, trying to get some kind of reaction out of her.

The rest of Clarissa was filling up with fear, making her back away, hands raised as if that would be enough to protect her.

"Look, I've had enough. I just want to go home. I don't even want the part, not if things are going to be like this!"

The figure kept advancing, lurching forward, playing his part.

Clarissa turned to run then, spinning on her heel. Impossibly, she found herself facing the bandaged man again. Somehow, he'd gotten behind her in an instant.

"Catch," he called, tossing the box of bullets to Clarissa.

She caught it without thinking, and in that moment, he leapt.

CHAPTER TWO

Exsanguination Killer Claims Another Victim

Those were the words on the news that had made Paige call Agent Sauer of the BAU last night, blurting out that she was accepting the job he'd offered her within his department of the FBI. He'd told Paige to call him back in the morning, obviously not wanting to trust in a decision made in the middle of the night.

Well, it was morning now in Washington. Time for Paige to either follow through or admit to herself that she had to be somewhere else, time for her to make up her mind.

She was staring into the bathroom mirror of her small apartment, trying to talk herself into making the call, one way or another. It was proving harder than she thought.

In the mirror, Paige could see the signs of stress contorting rounded features that were normally so youthful looking people had a hard time believing that she was twenty-five and a Ph.D. graduate. Her red hair was tangled because of all the times she'd unconsciously run her fingers through it, and the deep green of her eyes only seemed to reflect the worry Paige felt right then.

Should Paige just call Agent Sauer back and tell him that she'd made a mistake? Should she tell him that it was better to assign her to a field office, and for her to stay well clear of the BAU?

Not that Paige *wanted* to be anywhere else but D.C. It wasn't just her home; it was also the place where she had the best chances of finding answers in the one case that mattered most to her: her father's murder.

It was just that the whole situation with Christopher, Agent Marriott, made everything potentially far too complicated. Maybe too complicated to truly let her work alongside him. Paige couldn't deny that she felt a wave of attraction every time she looked at him. The kind of deep attraction that made her want to be near him, to say something, to *do* something about it.

Except that she couldn't, because Christopher was a married man. Paige had misread the signs. If he'd been friendly to her, and helped her, then it was just because he was working with her, not because of anything else. If he'd called her out of her FBI training to work alongside him, it was just because he respected her skills as a psychologist. Could Paige really work alongside Christopher now that she'd finished her training, torturing herself with his presence? She'd met his wife. Wouldn't she see Jennifer's face every time she looked over at Christopher and felt a hint of attraction?

Paige paced her small D.C. apartment, among the ornaments that she'd picked up in her time as a Ph.D. student, trying to make up her mind about something for which she thought she'd already made a decision last night.

The reasons for not working with Christopher were pretty compelling. It was just that there was at least one huge reason for doing it, and being a part of the BAU here.

Paige turned on the news, trying to find the story again. While the D.C. news cycle had pushed other stories about political wrangling and the economy to the top, the story that had caught Paige's attention was still there, with the news anchor looking grave as he started to read it.

"In other news, no new information has been released by the FBI on the so called 'Exsanguination Killer' case in Virginia, but they have confirmed that they will be working with local police to investigate the death of a young man who was found yesterday. Locally, the dead man has been tentatively identified as Terrence Williams, a senior at Virginia Tech, who was studying engineering."

Paige went over to her laptop and searched for the young man, trying to find out any details that might help her to add to her store of knowledge on the killer. She felt sure that if she could only find enough fragments of information, eventually it would lead to him. Inevitably, her search for his name brought wave after wave of news stories related to the murder, but since those were all basically saying that the FBI wasn't giving any information right now, it didn't help her much.

She found another story that made her hands clench into fists as she saw it: an explanatory piece on the Exsanguination Killer, one that talked about his previous crimes, setting out each one in turn. Paige couldn't stop herself from skimming it once she saw that it was there, even though she knew the details of the killer's crimes far better than the writer who had produced this online summary.

Twenty murders that people knew of, possibly more, in groups of three. A killer who ambushed his victims, drugged and bound them to stop them from fighting back, and then cut major veins, leaving them to bleed out slowly. The writer went through all of those details one by one with the kind of relish that made it hard for Paige to hold her anger in check. People's deaths shouldn't be entertainment.

Then she got to the profiles the site had produced on the killer's victims, each one set there with a photograph obviously scraped from social media, each one speculating on exactly what it was that had made them a target for the Exsanguination Killer. As someone who studied serial killers, Paige knew that was an important question. Often, it was possible to learn a lot about a killer by understanding why he chose one set of victims rather than another. She also understood that the wide variety of this serial killer's victims, men and women, younger and older, made him unusual.

Intellectually, Paige understood all of that, but seeing a picture of her father there among the others, seeing the article speculating about what he'd done to bring his own death down on him as if any of it were his fault… that was too much for her to handle.

In that moment, Paige was fourteen years old again, in the woods not far from the Virginia house she'd grown up in. She was looking down at her father's body again, seeing the blood, the strange pallor that had come over her father in death. Paige could feel the horror of that moment once more, as if she were experiencing it for the first time.

Bile rose up in her throat, and Paige ran for the bathroom; just the memory of that moment was enough to make her throw up. So much for being a tough, trained FBI agent now. It didn't matter that she'd had years of therapy. It didn't matter that she was a fully qualified psychologist. She didn't have control over that side of herself.

Paige went back to her computer, moving away from the sensationalist reports, and opening up her own files. She'd kept them since back before starting her Ph.D. on the minds of serial killers, adding small fragments to her notes every time she heard something that might relate to the man who had taken her father from her. Paige forced back her anger and horror now, forcing herself to add to those notes.

Feeling as though she was doing something that might eventually lead to finding the Exsanguination Killer was the closest thing to a coping mechanism Paige had managed to find for all of this. Her mother had relied on blotting things out, trying to move on and act as if it hadn't happened, ignoring the whole thing in the hope that eventually the pain would scab over, but Paige had never been able to do that. She'd never been able to understand her mother doing it, either.

Which meant that now, as with last night, there was no real choice to be made when it came to the offer that Agent Sauer had put in front of her. Yes, it would keep her away from Christopher. Yes, Paige could do good work in a field office somewhere. She could help to bring plenty of bad guys to justice. But it wouldn't be *this* bad guy, and this was the one who mattered to her more than any other. This was the reason she'd gone on to study serial killers. This was the reason she'd become an FBI agent.

Out in a field office, Paige wouldn't have any reason to work on this case as a part of her job. If she started accessing files, it would raise questions, and maybe even cost Paige her job for trying to pursue a personal agenda. She wouldn't have the full resources of the FBI behind her in her search.

As a member of the BAU, though, it would be her *job* to hunt for serial killers, and with this one having just struck, Paige would have every reason to look into the case. She had to be there, even if she knew that it was going to make things awkward between her and Christopher.

Paige was a grown woman; she could control herself around an attractive man. Even one who had saved her life at least once and who managed to be funny, intelligent and caring. She could be professional about all of this.

Paige swallowed as she realized just how difficult this might be, but she still picked up the phone to make the call to her soon-to-be boss.

"Sauer," a gruff voice on the other end of the line said, as if he couldn't be bothered to waste more words when just one would do.

"This is Paige King. I called you last night to accept your offer."

"Is this where you tell me that now you've slept on it, you've realized just what you're getting into, and you'd rather just have a normal job in a field office?" Agent Sauer asked.

He sounded as if it was something that he'd seen before. It was far too close to some of the things Paige had thought, but she pushed that aside. None of it mattered compared to her need to catch the Exsanguination Killer.

"No, I still want to be a part of the BAU," Paige said, getting the words out quickly so that she couldn't change her mind about any of it.

"That's good to hear, Paige," Agent Sauer said. "Of course, since you've already shown how well you work together, I'll be partnering you with Agent Marriott."

Paige resisted the urge to ask to work with someone else, because if she did that, she would have to explain the reason for it. Doing that would either make her look foolish and be written off immediately by Agent Sauer, or he would just tell her to work with Christopher anyway, and then the situation would be even more awkward. It was better not to say anything.

"That's good, sir," Paige said. "I'm eager to get started. I heard about the murder in Virginia. Is the BAU on that?"

She had to angle this around to the thing she most wanted to work on as quickly as possible.

"We are," Sauer said. "The preliminary reports are still coming through, so we don't want to jump to any conclusions yet, but we're working on the assumption that it is the Exsanguination Killer again, and not some kind of copycat."

Paige knew that her new boss was just being careful, not wanting to say anything for certain that wasn't supported by the evidence, but Paige knew it was the man who had killed her father. The similarities were too great. She could feel it.

"Was there anything this time that might move us closer to catching him?" Paige asked. She wanted every scrap of information that she could get on this. The killer who had changed her life was still out there, and Paige was determined to use this opportunity to get closer to him.

"We have CSI teams on the ground," Sauer said. "But obviously, this killer is good at leaving no traces of himself."

Paige knew that part. One reason for it was that the killer liked to kill outdoors, where rain, wind, and animal activity all combined to wipe away evidence. Another part seemed to be that the killer was careful, making sure that no one saw him, and that he left nothing behind that might lead back to him.

"Sir, if you want my help on this case, I've made a study of the killer as a part of my research," Paige said. She tried to make it sound as though it had all been for her Ph.D., and not because of an obsession that had begun with her father's death. She doubted that it would fool Sauer. He would have read her background checks, and would know exactly what relationship she had to this particular serial killer.

"I understand your interest in the case, Paige," Sauer said. "I know about your personal connection to it, but right now, that isn't the only case the FBI has to deal with. It isn't even the only serial killer. I have another situation that has come up that I believe you and Agent Marriott will be perfect for. Come over to our unit HQ in Quantico, and I'll fill you in."

He hung up without giving give Paige a chance to argue her case for inclusion on the Exsanguination Killer investigation. Paige doubted that it would have made much of a difference if he had. He'd clearly already made up his mind on it.

Which meant that Paige was going to have to spend her time looking into something else, something unrelated, while wondering if the FBI was getting any closer to the man who had murdered her father, and spending her time partnering with a man she really couldn't afford to get any closer to.

It was a combination that promised nothing but frustration, but Paige knew that she had to make the best of it. She'd made her choice now. She'd agreed to join the BAU, and a part of that was following orders, investigating where she was sent to investigate. She couldn't just turn around and say no because it wasn't the case she really wanted to look into. If this case was what Sauer wanted her to do, then it was what Paige was going to have to do. By working there, she was in the best place to hear what happened on the Exsanguination Killer case, and she would find a way to get more out of Sauer.

Paige raced to throw on her one smart suit. She needed to get to Quantico in a hurry.

CHAPTER THREE

Paige found her thoughts conflicted as she headed to Quantico, worried about Christopher and what would happen when Paige saw him again.

Quantico was around 35 miles from D.C., giving Paige plenty of time to think about what it would be like seeing Christopher again for the first time since her graduation from the FBI academy. For the first time since she'd met his *wife*.

That was the part that really had her rattled now, had her wondering if she could even do this. Before, Jennifer had been just someone Christopher mentioned in passing, still a reason for Paige to keep her distance but not enough to trigger this all-consuming worry. Now though, it felt as though even being in the same room as Christopher amounted to some kind of betrayal.

Paige didn't need her training as a psychologist to know that there was something deeper going on there, something that she was pushing back to avoid confronting it. That such an irrational reaction when she'd already told herself that nothing was going to happen with Christopher only spoke to the depth of the attraction that lay there towards him.

Paige just had to keep telling herself to put it from her mind. She had to focus. She had a briefing to attend, and a job to do.

It was strange to think that the actual town of Quantico had fewer than five hundred people living there, when the FBI campus held so many people, and the various military bases nearby held even more. The FBI facility was huge, with multiple buildings spread across at least a couple of square miles, encompassing everything from training facilities to state of the art labs and offices and firing ranges.

Paige had to stop her small electric car at a checkpoint, feeling a slight twinge of pride as she handed over her driver's license. She'd completed her training now. She wasn't a civilian consultant at a crime scene only because Christopher wanted her to be. She was an agent, and she was meant to be there.

"I'm looking for Agent Sauer and his division of the BAU," Paige said to the guard on the gate. Given the size of the FBI facility, she might spend hours wandering aimlessly before she found what she was looking for.

"Just over that way," the guard said, pointing. "Building thirteen."

Paige could only admire the scale of the whole place, and the modern construction of the building the guard had pointed out. It looked a little like the kind of building Paige was used to on a university campus, with ivy growing up the side and stone columns out front to lend it a sense of grandeur. Only the security measures around it said that it was more, from the bollards designed to prevent any kind of vehicular attack to the scanners set just beyond its large glass doors to pick up weapons or contraband.

It was a reminder to Paige of just how serious the situation she was stepping into was. This wasn't research that probably only a dozen people would read. This was work where lives might hang in the balance.

Paige made her way inside, and found Christopher waiting for her. The sight of him there made her pause, even though she'd known he was going to be there. He looked as boyishly handsome as always, six feet tall, with a square jaw, sandy hair, and blue eyes. His muscular frame was contained by a dark suit, the jacket open just enough to show the straps of the holster beneath.

"Paige," he said with a nod. It was polite and professional, but there wasn't something friendly and casual as there had been before between them. It was as if he could sense the awkwardness of Paige's attraction to him, pulling Paige in every direction all at once. "Sauer sent me down to welcome you and get you your equipment."

"My equipment?" Paige's head was spinning so much that it only really occurred to her then that, as an agent, there were things she would have to carry around with her that she wouldn't as a civilian. She could only follow in Christopher's wake as he led the way through to what appeared to be a small armory, where a large man in his forties stood waiting behind a screen. There were guns up on the wall, everything from assault rifles to sniper rifles, even what appeared to be a grenade launcher. There was enough ordnance there to supply a couple of military units, and seeing it all like that was a little overwhelming.

"Henry, it's Agent King here's first day. She needs your standard welcome package."

"All ready and waiting," the big man said. He slid something across the partition, setting it down as casually as if he'd done it a thousand times before. Paige realized that it was an official FBI badge and ID. She no longer had to wait for Christopher to show his, or explain that she was a psychologist or a trainee attached to an investigation. She could just say that she was with the FBI. That counted for a lot.

He pushed a holster and a sidearm across to Paige next. "This is a Glock 19M. You should be familiar with it from your training."

Paige was. She'd had to fire maybe 4000 rounds of ammunition downrange with one of these as part of her training, before she'd been taught to use shotguns and rifles. Her trainers had been clear: any qualified agent should be ready and able to use any weapon they needed to protect the public. It didn't matter if she was trying to become a profiler, she still had to be ready to do whatever was required.

Paige took the weapon and strapped it under her suit jacket. The final thing to hit the desk for her to take was a set of functional steel handcuffs. It was still sinking in for Paige that she could arrest people now, had a *responsibility* to arrest them, if it was necessary. All of this was a big step up from just helping out on investigations, and Paige had to admit that she felt a sense of trepidation as she took everything that was offered to her, putting it away carefully so that she could get to it if she needed it.

When she looked over at him, Christopher looked kind of proud, although the expression was gone again in an instant, and that didn't help Paige's determination to not react to him. She found that she *wanted* to make him proud. She wanted to impress him, wanted to make him think more of her, even though she knew that wasn't something she should be focusing on.

"Come on," he said. "Sauer is waiting for us."

He led the way to an elevator, and in that confined space, it was impossible for Paige not to pick up the sweet honeysuckle scent of his aftershave, not to focus on just how good he looked there. She just hoped that none of the ways she was reacting to Christopher were showing on her face.

Agent Sauer was waiting for them in a glass walled conference room on the third floor, standing in front of an evidence board on which he'd already pinned a couple of photographs. Both were of young women in their twenties, both pretty in their own ways, although they looked nothing alike to Paige. One was dark haired with high cheekbones and deep dark eyes, emphasized by heavy makeup, while the other was blonde and had a girl-next-door look, with slightly rounded features and a button nose, and a beauty mark on one cheek.

Agent Sauer was six feet tall and very slender, with a short dark beard and thin features. He glanced at a chrome plated watch as the two of them approached, and Paige couldn't tell if that was meant to imply that they were late, or if it was just a habit on his part, wanting to be precise about the time that everything happened.

"Agent Marriott. *Agent* King." He emphasized the word, obviously guessing that it was pretty much the first time anyone had called Paige that. "It's good that you're both here. We have something very serious going on in Las Vegas. The local police think that it's a serial killer, and they've asked for our help."

He gestured for them to take a seat at a broad mahogany conference table. Paige waited for Christopher to pick his seat so that she could sit a few chairs away from him, knowing that she needed to give herself the space when it came to him. If he noticed, he didn't show it.

"There have been two victims so far," Agent Sauer said. He pointed to the photograph of the dark haired woman. "This is Clarissa Bale. She was found dead in the middle of the stage of a Las Vegas theater this morning, with the spotlights pointing down at her. An empty box of prop bullets was found next to her. When the coroner moved in to examine her, they found that those bullets had been forced into her throat, suffocating her."

Paige saw Christopher wince at the news. "That's a nasty way to die. What about the other case?"

"That's Mylene Jacques," Sauer said. "She was also found suffocated on a stage, about a week ago. This time, though, it was because she had been locked in a giant safe. An airtight one."

Paige didn't get it. "If they were killed in such different ways, then why do the local police think that the two cases are connected?"

"They're both references to magic tricks," Christopher said. "The first is a reference to the bullet catch, and the second to an escapology effect."

He obviously caught Paige's look of surprise. "What? I know a little bit about magic."

Paige couldn't help herself as she heard that. She stared over at him. "You were that kid, weren't you?"

"What kid?"

"The kid every school has who's really into magic, and constantly trying to show people card tricks."

"I think I'll plead the fifth on that one," Christopher said, and for a moment or two it would have been easy to slide back into the easy banter that Paige had with him, but she realized that she couldn't do it. She couldn't risk it, because of how easily that could drift into something more. She forced herself to hold back.

"So bullets stuffed down the victim's throat and an airtight safe. Why would anyone need an airtight safe?"

"So that they can prove just how dangerous the trick they're performing is," Christopher said. "They show that the safe is airtight, and that means that they only have a limited time to escape."

Again, Paige found herself faintly impressed by the fact that he knew about all of this, even though it didn't really fit with what she already knew about him. It seemed that there were still plenty of facets to Christopher left to explore. Not that she should be the one exploring them.

"So, two young women killed in a week, using methods taken from magic tricks?" Paige said, trying to sum it up.

"The local police are sure it's one killer," Agent Sauer said, "and I agree. These deaths are just too weird for the two of them to be unrelated."

"Do we have background information on the two victims?" Christopher asked. "Details on their work, family, and lives? Anything the two of them might have in common?"

"I've put everything the local police and our techs have managed to find in the files," Agent Sauer said. "I'll forward them to your devices. Now, the two of you should get moving. I've already booked you both on a flight out of D.C., and arranged transport on the other end. I want you both in Vegas as soon as possible. With a killer like this, there's far too much of a risk that he might try to kill again soon."

"I'll grab my go-bag," Christopher said, heading out of the conference room in a hurry without so much as a glance back at Paige.

Paige didn't have a go-bag, hadn't thought that she might need something like that. Maybe there would be enough time for her to run home and pack what she would need on the way to the airport. Failing that, she was just going to have to buy what she needed in Las Vegas.

For now, though, Paige had another concern. She was alone with Agent Sauer in person, and she still wanted to know everything that had happened with the new murder that had been attributed to the Exsanguination Killer, even if she wasn't going to be assigned to that case. She still wanted to get any scrap of information she could about the case.

"Sir," Paige said. "About the other murder, the one in Virginia…"

"We have people working on that, Agent King," Agent Sauer said, in a firm tone.

"I know that, sir, but-"

"I need you to focus on the case you've been assigned," her boss said. "If you want to discuss it after you get back, then we can, but for now, I need you to get to Las Vegas. You have a serial killer to catch."

He had a point. The killer was turning his murders into performances, and now that he'd succeeded in grabbing the FBI's attention, how much longer would it be before he struck again?

CHAPTER FOUR

Paige was a little surprised by the speed with which they rushed down to the airport, definitely not leaving any time to pack. She and Christopher were hurried through airport security, their badges letting them move quicker than the usual line.

It meant that Paige got more time in her seat with her laptop balanced in front of her, more time in which to pull up the files and try to get a head start on the case.

"We'll probably have some time when we land for you to do that," Christopher pointed out.

Paige was all too aware of his presence in the seat next to her. Close enough that she could reach out and touch his hand if she wanted…

Except that doing so would be a very bad idea. He was her partner, not anything else.

"I want to be sure that I've got as much of it in my head as I can," Paige said. "I can't help if I don't have all the information."

"It's not about helping anymore, Paige," Christopher pointed out. "You're a fully trained agent now. This is your case as much as mine. I'm not here to hold your hand."

Those words hit Paige all at once. She was used to a dynamic between the two of them where she did everything she could to help solve the case, but ultimately, Christopher was the agent working it. He was the one with the responsibility to succeed, and he was the one making the final decisions. Whether people lived or died came down to him. Now, even though he was still the senior agent in their little partnership, Paige was every bit as responsible for succeeding in this as he was.

"All the more reason to make sure I'm on top of everything," Paige said. There was another part to it too: if she focused on the work, then it was easier to ignore the potential difficulty of thinking about the attraction between her and Christopher.

"Ok," Christopher said. "Just make sure that there isn't some kid looking over your shoulder at all of the crime scene photographs."

He had a serious point. Much of what was in the police reports wouldn't be for public consumption. There would be details in there that the FBI would want to hold back, and certainly, it wouldn't be right for just anyone to stare at pictures of the dead women.

That meant Paige had to hunch in over the screen as she started to read, trying to shield it from view as the plane took off and winged its way towards Las Vegas. By this point, there were crime scene reports, files from the coroner, lists of evidence, and whatever the FBI techs had been able to scrape from the social media accounts of the victims.

It was all raw data at this point, but Paige was used to sorting through large bodies of information, trying to find the threads hidden beneath. She'd done it when she was a research student, interviewing serial killers for her Ph.D., trying to understand them and what motivated them. Of course, there, one of them had escaped and tried to kill the people around her because he thought that she could be just like him.

This killer had killed two people so far that they knew about: Clarissa Bale and Mylene Jacques. Both were young women in their twenties, both were lovely, and maybe that pointed to the start of a victim profile for Paige, except that the two women were too dissimilar for it to be that simple. They didn't look alike, and they worked different jobs. Clarissa was an aspiring actress, while Mylene worked in sales. They both lived in Vegas, but in different areas: Clarissa in a shared apartment, Mylene in a suburban home on the fringes of the city. None of those things seemed to be what the killer was focusing on.

Paige tried running searches on their social media, trying to establish if the two of them had any connection with one another. They didn't seem to be friends or followers on any of each other's accounts, but that wasn't enough for Paige. She looked for any places they'd checked in that the two had in common, trying to find any context in which the two might have met one another.

More importantly, trying to find any context in which the killer might have found both of them. If Paige could find spots where they'd both been, then maybe that would give her and Christopher somewhere to start searching for any evidence of someone following them there.

It might also point to someone who simply had a reason to hate both of them. With only two victims so far, it didn't necessarily mean that they were dealing with a classic serial killer, in spite of the bizarre methods used in the murders. It could just be a guy who had broken up with both of them, or a woman who thought they'd both gotten jobs that she should have had.

The only problem was that Paige couldn't find anywhere that they'd both hung out. Any point of connection between them at all. Maybe they'd both gone to the same show once, or the same mall, but Paige couldn't see any evidence of it, certainly not recently.

And it would *be* recent. This was a killer who'd embarked on a sudden spree, with kills close together. While the roots of that might be years in the making, Paige had the feeling that the trigger would be more recent. That meant that he would have looked for his victims more recently too. Maybe that search represented a chance to find him, but only if Paige could work out a spot where he might have found both his victims, or the criteria he was using to pick them.

Because there didn't seem to be anything in the files that could give her that part, Paige decided to switch her approach, trying to focus on the crimes and the methods involved.

She looked over the crime scene photographs, trying to spot anything in them that stood out as unusual. Of course, since both murders mimicked magic tricks, there was plenty that was unusual there. It was just a question of what was relevant.

The reports gave roughly the same details that Agent Sauer had set out for her and Christopher back in Quantico. Paige felt a sense of growing horror as she looked over the photographs, seeing the dead women lying there, Clarissa in the middle of a stage, Mylene hunched up inside a safe. Both of them pale and panicked looking, eyes wide as they fought for their last breaths. There wasn't the blood that Paige had seen at other crime scenes, wasn't the physical damage, but the sight of the women dead there like that was still more than enough to make her recoil in horror.

Paige was grateful for that sense of horror, in a way. After all the time she'd spent working with serial killers, and all the things she'd seen in the last couple of cases she'd worked with Christopher, Paige had started to worry that she might become inured to the violence. She had started to worry that she might not feel anything anymore, that she might become something as empty and dead inside as some of the killers she chased. She didn't want that. She didn't ever want to stop seeing just how vile it was that two young women had been killed like this.

Paige took a second or two to swallow back her horror. It was one thing to feel it, quite another to be overwhelmed by it to the extent that she couldn't do her job as a federal agent. She needed to do the work here, needed to find the killer for these victims, and for all the others who might die if Paige didn't find the killer in time.

She found herself staring at the photographs of the victims again, trying to pick out any details she could. There were close up shots of their faces, discolored by death, eyes wide and staring. Clarissa Bale was wearing heavy makeup.

Why the makeup? It was possible that it was simply what she wore every day, but combined with her figure hugging dress, Paige didn't think so. Was she going on a date when she was killed? Was she on a night out with friends, or coming back from some kind of event? No, Paige realized, those weren't the only options. Clarissa was trying to be an actress, so maybe this counted as her preparing for an audition. Maybe she was just trying to look her best in the hope of being picked for a part.

"Christopher," Paige said. "Do we have anything that points to Clarissa Bale having been given an audition for something?"

"Maybe in her messages or email?" Christopher suggested, without looking up.

Paige looked through, and found an email.

Dear Clarissa,

Thank you for your response, and for your portfolio. We think you might be a good fit for the show we're building, and would like to see you to audition this Tuesday. Because we have shows running during the day, we have to run the auditions later at night. I hope that won't be a problem for you. We've booked a slot for you to audition at 11:45.

That probably helped to narrow down the time of death, but it also potentially gave them another route to the killer. One that might let them catch him quickly, maybe even before Paige and Christopher hit the ground.

"Christopher, presumably we have ways to trace this email back to the person who sent it?" Paige said.

"I think our tech people are trying, but it looks like it's from a burner account, set up just for this. Maybe we'll be able to trace it back to a phone or a computer in a café somewhere, but then linking it back to a specific person might be harder."

"I guess it was too much to hope that this guy would be stupid enough to send the email from his own account," Paige said.

"If it were that simple, then they wouldn't need us to catch him," Christopher said. "But we'll think of something."

He sounded so confident about that, either because of the cases they'd worked on before, or simply because he trusted in their talents. Paige wished that she had that kind of confidence, the kind that came from working case after case, catching criminal after criminal.

"I hope so," Paige said.

"I have you here," Christopher said, as if that made all the difference, turning it into a near certainty. "Have you worked out anything about the killer yet?"

He said it as if he assumed that Paige would have them fully profiled by now. Paige tried to think, looking at the crime scene photographs. What did the things they knew about the murders tell them about the killer? What could Paige deduce about him?

"The MO is the most interesting part of it," Paige said. "You said that he killed both victims in ways that mimic existing magic tricks?"

Christopher nodded. "The bullet catch and a standard escapology trick."

"Explain to me how the tricks are meant to work," Paige said, partly because she wanted to understand more about the killer, and partly because she wanted to see just how much Christopher knew about all this.

"There are different versions of both," Christopher said. "But there are kind of standard, classic versions."

He really did sound as if he knew a lot about magic. Paige found herself wondering if his knowledge was just a hangover from when he was a kid, or something he still had an interest in.

"Tell me about those," Paige said.

"For the bullet catch, the magician calls an audience member up on stage and has them mark or initial a bullet," Christopher said, with sudden enthusiasm. "They put that bullet in a gun, and an assistant, or sometimes the audience member, fires it at the magician. The magician then reveals the bullet that was signed, held between their teeth. Although in the original version, it was caught in a plate."

Paige had to admit that it was fun watching him geek out about a subject he obviously knew well. She had to remind herself that this wasn't about watching Christopher's reactions, though. This was about trying to catch a killer.

"And the prop bullets?" Paige said.

Christopher looked suddenly serious. "Chung Ling Soo died performing the trick when his specially altered rifle misfired, shooting the real bullet, rather than a blank round. Or maybe a worn fragment.

Opinion is divided. What we know is that more people have died doing this one trick than any other. These days, there are versions of the trick using dummy bullets to try to increase the safety."

Again, Paige could see the way his face lit up when he was talking about something he obviously knew about. It was hard not to feel a wave of attraction as that life came into him.

"What about the trick with the safe?" Paige asked him, forcing herself to focus on the case.

"That's more about escapology than classic magic," Christopher said. He sounded as if it wasn't something he gave quite as much attention to.

"Not the kind of thing you do?" Paige asked him, suddenly wanting to know more about him.

Christopher looked slightly embarrassed. "I mostly just do card tricks and sleight of hand. Close up magic."

"Ah, so you admit you still do it!" Paige said, suddenly aware of how easy it was to add this layer of friendliness above the professionalism. Too easy, maybe, because it would be simple to slide into more than that, into thinking that there was more there than there was.

"Ok, yes," Christopher admitted. He took out his FBI badge, put it between his hands, an in an instant it was gone, vanished.

Paige had to fight the urge to applaud. She had to focus on the case, not on Christopher.

"Do you know how the safe trick works?" Paige asked.

Christopher nodded. "The performer or assistant is tied up, handcuffed, sometimes placed in a sack, and then locked inside a safe. The idea is for them to try to escape before a set time. Having a safe that can be demonstrated to be airtight ups the sense of peril. In some versions, they just escape, but it's more common for them to leave it until the audience members are panicking, then open the safe to show that they've disappeared."

So in both cases, the killer had chosen to copy classic magic tricks, but it wasn't so much about the magic angle as about what that could tell them about the killer.

"What interests me is that he chose two different tricks to copy," Paige said. "Serial killers can be incredibly specific about their methods sometimes. The method becomes like a ritual that has to be performed precisely. But this one has used two very different ones here. The magic trick side of this seems like the only unifying factor."

"So do you think we're actually looking for a magician?" Christopher asked.

"It seems likely," Paige replied. "The magic has to be meaningful to the killer, otherwise why go to all of that trouble? Those are some pretty elaborate lengths he went to in order to do things this way rather than… I don't know, sneaking up and stabbing someone."

But he couldn't do that, because that didn't fit with whatever was going on inside his head. No, all of this meant something to the killer, something deeply personal. Something that meant so much that he couldn't do things any other way. Finding out exactly what might be the key that allowed the two of them to unlock the whole case.

"Hopefully, that narrows down the suspect pool a little," Christopher said. "Although, in Vegas, maybe not as much as we'd like. Stage magic is huge there. A Las Vegas show is seen as the pinnacle of a lot of magicians' careers."

"And now, here's a serial killer putting on his own kind of performance there for the world to see," Paige said. Could that be what this was? A way for someone to get the attention they felt they deserved? A way to grab the eyes of the world when they hadn't been able to in a normal way?

"Do you think that's what this is about?" Christopher asked.

"I think it's possible," Paige replied. "And I think there's an element of control to all of this as well. A magic trick puts the magician in a position of power, where they control what the audience sees and does. They control their assistants, the circumstances, all of it. Maybe this is a way of someone expressing a wish to take control of events in their life in the most violent way possible."

"So an out of control magician," Christopher said.

Paige shrugged. "I still want to know more. When we get to Las Vegas, we need to take a closer look at the most recent crime scene."

CHAPTER FIVE

They drove over to the theater in a car that was waiting for them at the airport. It obviously wasn't a rental, though, because Paige could see the lights and sirens hidden beneath the grill, and when she opened up the trunk, she found tactical gear waiting there for her and Christopher. It seemed like the local field office had left it ready for them.

As they drove through the city, Paige found her eyes drawn to the endless bright lights and spectacle of the place, every inch of Las Vegas seeming to scream for attention all at once. There were huge billboards advertising the latest shows, and recreations of landmarks of the world, from the Eiffel Tower to Egyptian pyramids. The bulk of casinos rose on either side, each seeming to compete to be larger and more extravagant than its neighbors. The sheer scale of it all was kind of overwhelming.

"The strip is a lot to take in," Christopher said as he drove. He seemed to have guessed what Paige was thinking. Maybe it was just because it was impossible *not* to think that way in a place as over the top as this, or maybe because he was just paying that kind of attention to her.

"I'm just wondering if all of this fed into the way the killer is committing his crimes," Paige said. "If everything around here is shouting for attention, maybe he feels as though he needs to do something elaborate to have any kind of impact on the city?"

"So you think this is about attention?" Christopher asked. He sounded as if he wasn't sure that was enough.

Paige wasn't sure what to think right then. "Possibly. I think that it has to be a part of it, but I don't know if it's the whole thing or not. This killer has to know that killing in such an extravagant way will get media attention, but is that the only point to this? There are a lot of ways of committing spectacular crimes. I feel as though the magic angle has to be more personal to him than that."

They were sliding off the strip now, into streets filled with smaller theaters and casinos, ones that still tried to pull in crowds with the gaudiness of their facades, but didn't quite manage the same brightness or extravagance. In comparison, these theaters looked almost cheap, the shows they advertised featuring second rate singers and comedians. Several advertised magic shows, so Paige started to realize just what a big deal magic was in Vegas. How many magicians were there here? Even if they could be certain that this was a magician, and not just one of the many people out there with an interest in magic, the pool of suspects would still be too large for that to be enough to find the killer.

The theater they wanted was easy enough to find, if only because the presence of the police around it stood out even against the busy background of the city, proclaiming what had happened to the world. There were squad cars parked in front of it, along with a van for CSI techs. Police tape cordoned off the space in front of the theater, making it clear that the musical it was currently showing wouldn't be running today.

There was still a crowd, though, standing around and staring, as if this were just one more facet to the entertainment of the city. Quite a lot of them seemed to be reporters.

Paige and Christopher parked, then hurried up to that tape, keeping their heads down so that the reporters wouldn't have a chance to ask too many questions. There was a faint thrill for Paige at being able to flash her badge there, letting the cop on duty know that she was an agent. It was more than offset by the worry that came from the fact that she was about to step into an active crime scene, into the space where a young woman had been murdered.

Paige had to remind herself that she had done that before. She could handle this. She *had* to handle this.

"The main stage is that way," the officer said, pointing. "That's where she was found."

"Thanks," Christopher said. "Who's the detective assigned to the case on your side?"

"That would be Detective Renard," the cop said. "Although he's back at the precinct now. I can call him if you like."

Paige saw Christopher shake his head, though. Quickly, like he was determined not to give the cop a chance to do it. "We'll catch up with him later."

Paige got the feeling that he wanted to do this part of things alone. She understood that the relationship between the FBI and local police could sometimes be complicated. Maybe Christopher wanted to keep this part as simple as possible, without the addition of a detective who might get in the way? Or maybe Christopher just wanted to get a good look at the crime scene before talking to the local cops.

Either way, he headed inside and Paige had to follow him into the depths of the theater, into a large auditorium that could easily have seated a couple of thousand people on rows of folding red velvet seats. Gilded stucco ornaments on the ceiling and faux marble pillars leant a baroque feel to the place, giving Paige the impression that it was trying to be more upmarket than it actually was, without quite succeeding. A CSI team moved around the stage in their white plastic evidence suits, using brushes and blacklights on the corners of the stage so that it looked like a silent performance of their job.

One man obviously wasn't with the police. He was a large man in his fifties, who wore a shiny cheap suit that looked as though he'd worn it a few too many times. He had short-cropped hair, and his features looked as though he'd started off handsome before he'd been in a few fights somewhere along the line. It didn't help that he also had dark rings under his eyes, as if worry or lack of sleep were starting to get to him.

Paige took a guess, based on a combination of the way he looked and the simple fact that he stood in the middle of it all, looking it over the way another man might have looked at contractors working in his house.

"Are you the manager here?" she asked, because it was the only reason she could think of that he might have behaved like that.

"Are you more cops?" he demanded. "How many more of you are there going to be before I can open my theater again?"

"We're FBI," Christopher said. "I'm Agent Marriott, this is Agent King. Now, are you the manager, sir?"

He repeated Paige's question slightly more firmly.

"FBI now? Let me guess, you're going to want to start everything from the top, and I'm going to be closed for another day."

Paige could hear the frustration there, presumably at the effect all of this was having on his bottom line. Still, that seemed pretty callous when someone had just been murdered in his establishment. Maybe it was just his way of dealing with the shock of it all, trying to shut it out, the way her mother had when her father died.

"Don't you care that someone was killed here?" Paige asked.

"Of course I care," the man said. "I care that some sicko chose here to do something like that. I care that I walked in this morning and almost had a heart attack when I saw all this. I also care about the fact that if this goes on much longer, I'll have to start canceling performances. Do you know how tight the margins are with a magic show that's not on the strip? Do you know how many people lose their jobs if the run falls through?"

"The sooner you help us, the sooner we'll be gone," Christopher said.

Paige wondered if it would actually be that simple. The CSI team would presumably keep working on the scene until they were sure that there was no more evidence to be gathered. Certainly, they wouldn't allow a whole audience to trample through the theater and contaminate the crime scene until then. That probably meant that the theater would be closed for days.

Still, she understood what Christopher was doing. If this man was mostly worried about the risk of the theater being closed, that was good motivation for him to give them all the information that he could.

"Why don't we start over?" Paige suggested. "We still don't have your name, sir."

"Evans," the big man replied. "Andrew Evans. This is my theater. At least, I manage it."

"And you were the one to find the body this morning?" Christopher said, obviously catching Evans's comment about nearly having a heart attack.

"Like I said, I walked in, and I saw it. Saw *her*."

There was a flicker of pain in his voice, and now Paige wondered if his eagerness to get all of this over with might be a coping mechanism, if he was trying to just get through it because the thought of what he'd seen disturbed him too much. Maybe this wasn't all about the money for him.

"Can you walk us through that?" Christopher said. "What was the theater like when you walked in? Were the doors locked? Was it dark, or were the lights on?"

"The stage door was unlocked when I showed up," Evans said. "And there were spotlights pointing down at the stage. There was a mirror set up on it too that shouldn't have been there. That was when I saw… her."

Paige felt a moment of sympathy for him, having to see something like that. Paige knew from experience just how difficult it could be.

She also found herself looking over to the stage. A large mirror was still set up there, at the foot of the stage, angled upwards. Paige frowned, not quite understanding.

"Is this another part of the trick?" she asked.

Christopher was also frowning. "This is a different trick, mixed in. It's one called Pepper's Ghost. It uses carefully angled mirrors to make the magician appear to be somewhere they're not. It's even older than the bullet catch."

Paige guessed that it would have meant that Clarissa Bale didn't know which direction the attack was coming from until it was too late.

She returned her attention to the theater manager.

"Tell us more about what you saw when you came in," she said. "Was it usual for the lights to be on like that?"

"I thought that someone had come in for some kind of early rehearsal, or maybe Lucas had come in for one of his late night hookups and left the lights on."

"Late night hookups?" Paige said. There hadn't been anything about that in the file.

"One of the stagehands likes to bring girls back here after hours," the manager said. "He thinks it impresses them more than his apartment, or maybe he just doesn't like them knowing where he lives. He swiped a key from my stage manager a couple of years back and I never got around to changing it."

"Or firing him," Paige said. "You don't mind him stealing from you?"

She saw the manager shrug.

"He's good at his job and he does anything that needs doing while he's here, so it works out for me," the manager said.

"Do all of your employees get to use the theater after hours?" Christopher asked.

"Of course not," Evans said. "You think I'm just going to give everyone who wants one a key to this place?"

"So who *does* have keys?" Paige asked.

Evans looked a little put out by the question. "What? You're going to start accusing my staff of something like this? Isn't it obvious that someone broke in to do this?"

Christopher shook his head. "Like you said, you found the door unlocked. Had it been damaged? Forced open?"

Evans shook his head. "No, I guess not."

"So who had keys?" Paige pressed him.

That got another shrug from the manager. "At this point, it's just me and Lucas. One or the other of us is always here to open up or lock up."

Which reduced the pool of potential suspects considerably, assuming a key had really been used.

"Where were you last night, Mr. Evans? An hour either side of midnight?"

"What? I'm a suspect now?" He sounded slightly offended by that.

"We just need to eliminate you from our inquiry," Paige said. "The sooner we do that, the sooner we can be out of your hair and let you open up again."

That seemed like the best incentive to offer him right then.

"I was watching the fights over at the Chester Casino. It was a good card. I'm friends with the owner. We had a few drinks. I was there until maybe two."

"We'll need contact details for your friend," Christopher said.

It was obvious to Paige though that he wasn't particularly interested in Mr. Evans as a suspect now that he'd produced the possibility of an alibi. Nor, honestly, was Paige. She was convinced that the sight of the murder scene horrified him, even if he was hiding it well.

The stagehand with after-hours access to the theater was a different matter. A man who viewed this place as his own private spot, and who liked to bring women here while no one was around? A man who worked in the theater, and who had presumably helped to set up plenty of magical effects, given the show that was going on? That sounded like someone who might easily have the means to do this.

"Tell us about Lucas," Paige said.

"There's not much to say. He does his job."

"You've never had any trouble with him?" Christopher asked.

Evans shrugged. "He comes and goes at odd hours. He doesn't always show up when he's meant to. We had a couple of complaints from women about the way he's hit on them, I guess."

"You guess?" Paige said. "Did you or didn't you?"

"Well, yes," Evans said. "I just didn't figure it was that big a deal."

Unless it was more than that. Whether he had a motive or the kind of obsession with magic that would be required remained to be seen, but at the very least, he was someone who might have seen something, someone to whom Paige and Christopher definitely needed to talk more.

"Where can we find this 'Lucas' now?" Paige asked. "We'll need his full name and as good a description as you can give us."

"Lucas Francisco. He has a day job over at the Illustrious," Evans said. "It's a casino over on the strip. I have a photograph of him somewhere."

Then that was where they needed to go next. If Lucas was the only other person with a key to the theater, then they needed to speak to him at once.

CHAPTER SIX

"Is everything all right?" Christopher asked.

"Yes, everything's fine," Paige assured him, possibly a little too quickly.

Paige wasn't sure what to say to Christopher as the two of them drove over to the Illustrious. She knew that she ought to talk to him about the case, go through all the possibilities that might allow them to find the killer they were looking for.

It should have been easy; instead, Paige was wary of saying anything in case she said the wrong thing, in case she said something that crossed one of the invisible lines that were suddenly there between her and Christopher. Lines that she'd put in place the moment she knew he was taken.

"Are you sure?" he asked. "It's just that you've been pretty quiet ever since we set off from D.C."

"I'm just thinking about the case," Paige said. It was hard to pretend that everything was normal. "Do you think Lucas Francisco is a good suspect for this?"

"Do you have doubts?" Christopher asked. "He's one of two people with after-hours access to the theater, and if he's worked there on their magic shows, he might have the connections to get what he needs for the tricks."

"He might," Paige said. "And we have to follow up, but isn't it possible that there were other ways someone got into the theater? If someone is really that into escapology, wouldn't they be able to pick a lock?"

"They would," Christopher agreed, and that meant that none of this was certain. "But we still need to run this down. Lucas might be our killer, and if he is, then we need to get to him before he has a chance to kill again. At the very least, we need to talk to him and eliminate him as a suspect."

That was true. They needed to follow whatever evidence there was. Maybe Lucas *was* the killer. At the very least, he might have seen something. A guy who was often there late at night? Maybe he'd swung by last night and spotted the killer, or a piece of evidence that might lead them to him.

The Illustrious was a significant move up in class from the theater where Lucas worked at night. Its broad front dominated a large section of the strip, lit up even during the day as if any pause in the brightness would lose it customers. It rose high above, a hotel sitting there above the casino on the ground floor, rising up to blot out the sky. The whole place was made to look almost deliberately old-fashioned, like some high class French hotel, while the grounds in front had been turned into something like an eighteenth century formal garden.

Paige and Christopher pulled up in front and a valet went to take their keys. Paige saw Christopher hesitate, obviously not wanting the car to be far away if they needed it, or not wanting the government vehicle to be in the hands of someone else, but there didn't seem to be any other real choice here.

"Keep it close by," he said to the attendant, flashing his badge.

"Yes sir," the attendant said, and the two of them headed inside.

The interior was, if anything, even more opulent than the exterior had been. The whole place gave the impression of having been intricately carved from walnut and marble, forming a seamless whole. The reception desk looked not so much built from marble as almost extruded from the shining gloss of the floor. Signs pointed the way to half a dozen different convention rooms and auditoriums, while a broad casino floor spread out in every direction, so that it would be necessary to walk through it to get anywhere there.

There were displays set up around the floor of the casino, obviously designed to catch the eyes of anyone there so that they would stop long enough to get caught up in the gambling. There were modern looking statues and art installations, chandeliers that looked as though each had been individually designed, even a large tank with a walkway running around it, in which swam what appeared to Paige to be small sharks. Each gaming table featured a dealer dressed in black slacks, a white shirt, and a waistcoat that featured gold swirls on a black background, all dressed identically, so that it was hard to tell one from another at a distance.

It was about then that Paige realized that finding Lucas would be anything but simple, even when they had a photograph to work with. A place like this would have hundreds, maybe even thousands, of guests and gamblers. Finding one man in all of this would take forever.

"We're looking for Lucas Francisco," Christopher said to the receptionist on the front desk and showing his badge. "We're told that he works here."

"I can check for you," the receptionist said, in a polite, professional tone. "What's all this about?"

"We need to talk to him in connection to an ongoing investigation," Christopher said. Obviously he wouldn't mention the murder. That would only cause the kind of trouble that they didn't need.

"I have him on the system now," the receptionist said. "The locations for all of our dealers are logged, for security."

"For security?" Paige said, not quite understanding.

"If there are losses, the house likes to know what table they're coming from," the receptionist explained. "Anyway, it looks like he's dealing blackjack on table 15, over that way."

She gestured to a spot in the casino, with its rows of tables and slot machines filled with gamblers.

There was still the matter of covering the space between where they stood and the table at which Lucas was dealing. Stepping into the casino was like plunging into an overwhelming sea of light and noise, with dealers calling out wins and losses, slot machines ringing out with wins and losses, customers cursing their luck. It was so all consuming that it was almost impossible to keep track of which direction they were moving in.

Paige's eyes weren't on the tables as she passed. Instead, she found herself watching the faces of the people there, taking in the hope, the elation, the pain and the desperation there, reading their expressions and their body language automatically. She saw the tired expressions of people who had obviously been in there for hours at a time, gambling without stopping, and picked out the ones who were probably slightly tipsy on free drinks to make any kind of good decisions.

She watched Christopher's eyes roving the room and guessed that he was looking for very different things from her. She saw him glance over to where the casino's security guards stood here and there in the crowd, watching over proceedings as discretely as possible. She also saw him glance towards the dark domes of security cameras set around the room. He was obviously watching for threats, assessing the extent of the security in the place, and trying to pick out Lucas from the other dealers.

He led the way, his larger frame forging a path that Paige could follow across the casino floor. She had to sidestep as a particularly bulky man eased his way from one slot machine to another, but quickly caught up again, falling into step behind him.

Paige could see that each of the tables had a discretely placed number on its side in raised gold lettering. They offered a mixture of different games, as if set up to allow people bored with one table to move quickly and easily to spend their money at another.

Table fifteen was about halfway across the hall, not far from the giant tank with its collection of small sharks swimming slowly around and around. Paige and Christopher made their way to it, and as they walked up to the table, Paige found herself staring at the man dealing cards crisply and smoothly to a quartet of gamblers.

He was in his thirties, with short blonde hair and lean features. He was slender, barely filling out his uniform. His long fingered hands moved quickly and confidently on the cards, making them skim out over the table like stones skipping across water, coming to rest neatly in front of each of the gamblers sitting there.

He looked up as they approached, flashing a professional looking smile their way, as if he'd done it with dozens of potential gamblers already that day. "We have a couple of spare seats if you'd like me to deal you in."

"We're not here for that," Christopher said. He flashed his badge, and in that moment, Paige saw the change in Lucas Francisco's expression. She saw the fear there, and the sudden flash of determination.

"He's going to run!" Paige called out, but she was an instant too late in shouting it. Lucas was already on his feet, sending stacks of casino chips scattering.

He darted around the table, and Paige set off after him, trying to grab him before he could get away. She was an agent now, and that meant that she couldn't hang back, leaving this kind of thing to Christopher. Not that she ever had.

Christopher was running at Lucas from the other side of the table, the two of them converging in a pincer movement that should have been enough to trap him. Instead, though, he leapt up onto the table, kicking cards in every direction as he made a run into the midst of the casino.

Paige set off in pursuit. She was aware of the weight of her gun at her side, and had a split second to decide whether to use it, having to weigh up all the factors that her instructors had tried to drill into her in an instant. Paige decided against it. This was an unarmed suspect in the middle of a room full of people who might be hit if Paige missed. Both of those things meant that she needed to chase, not reach for her weapon.

Paige sprinted after the fleeing figure of Lucas, dodging left and right to try to make her way through the crowd in the casino at speed. Christopher was pushing his way through much more directly, not giving the other man a chance to get away. Paige could see, though, that they weren't going to be able to get close to him through the crowd.

She cut around instead, trying to get in front of Lucas so that he would have nowhere left to run. Paige ran along the line of slot machines, hearing one paying out even as she ran past. That slowed her down because an older woman came out in front of her with her hands in the air, beaming with joy, and Paige had to sidestep to avoid knocking her over as she ran.

She could see Christopher still chasing after Lucas, and Paige was in front of them both now. She swung around in front of the path she thought Lucas was going to take, moving into place to try to tackle him as he came close to her.

He spotted her. But because Paige had cut off his other options, there were only so many places he could go. He changed course, heading for a flight of metal stairs that led to the raised walkway above the shark tank that Paige had seen when she came in. Paige followed, determined not to let him get away.

Paige followed him up the steps to the walkway, with Christopher just a pace or so behind. They were up well above the casino floor now, and the shark tank was there just the other side of a short railing.

Lucas started to back away along the walkway, obviously looking for a spot where he could drop down to the casino floor again safely, leaving Paige and Christopher behind. He looked panicky, obviously determined to do whatever it took not to be caught. Before, Paige had doubts about whether he was the murderer, but seeing him do this much to get away, she had to admit he was looking more and more like he might be involved after all.

"Lucas, you need to stop," she said, trying to talk him down. "There's nowhere for you to go. We just want to talk to you."

As she talked, she moved around the walkway, cutting off his options for escape. Paige was doing her best to defuse the situation, not wanting to escalate into violence up here, but Lucas was still backing away.

"You think I'm falling for that?" he demanded.

Paige kept advancing. "You need to stay where you are, Lucas."

He was getting close to the railing now, but he didn't seem to notice the danger.

"Leave me alone, or-"

Paige never got to find out what Lucas's threat was going to be, because that was the moment when his foot slipped on his next backward step. He reached out to try to balance, but there was nothing to support him. He went straight over the railing, arms pinwheeling as he tumbled into the tank with a splash that sent water flying up into the air.

The small sharks within scattered out of the way of the sudden falling form, and Lucas came flailing to the surface, spluttering as he did so, flailing and trying to swim.

The small sharks seemed to have gotten over their initial shock, and were nosing around Lucas, nudging against him as if trying to judge whether he was small enough to eat.

"Get me out of here!" Lucas cried out.

There was a net by the side of the tank, obviously used for cleaning it. Paige grabbed for it, holding it out for Lucas to hold onto. Christopher was there with her then, pulling him in to the side of the tank and then hauling him out of it. He lay there, soaked and panting as he stared up at the ceiling.

"Lucas Francisco," Christopher said. "We'd like to ask you some questions."

CHAPTER SEVEN

Pretty much from the moment that Christopher hauled Lucas Francisco down from the walkway around the tank, casino staff were there, all trying to talk at once.

"What's going on?" one man who looked like he might be a manager demanded, in an unhappy tone. "Look at the chaos you've caused!"

"Security!" another dealer called out. "Someone's attacking our dealers! Why isn't security dealing with this?"

Security guards were indeed coming forward, four of them converging the way they might have on a card counter or an aggressive drunk in the middle of the casino. Christopher had his ID out as they approached, holding it up to ward them off even as he and Paige continued to march Lucas through the casino.

"FBI," he said in a firm tone, wanting to make it very clear that he wasn't about to allow any trouble here. If the casino security did think that someone had randomly attacked one of their dealers, then Christopher suspected that they wouldn't hesitate to use violence.

"FBI?" the manager said. "The *FBI* are causing chaos on my casino floor? Do you know how much damage you've done?"

Christopher looked around pointedly. As far as he could see, there *wasn't* any real damage.

"Every hand knocked over is money lost!" the manager complained. "And those chips everywhere? There's no way of knowing who's picked them up."

"You're worried about money at a time like this?" Paige asked, sounding as if she couldn't quite believe it.

Christopher could, because he understood how strange people's priorities could get when they were put under stress. Paige knew about people, Christopher *knew* how much she knew, but she didn't have his experience yet of stressful, dangerous situations.

She hadn't hesitated, though, when Lucas had tried to make a run for it. She'd actually been the one to catch up to him first. She wasn't just proving that she was good enough to be an agent, she was doing it better than Christopher was. It was… very impressive.

He couldn't afford to focus on her right then, though. Or at all. He had to focus on the case, and on dealing with the situation in front of him. He had a suspect to question, and he was determined to get answers.

"This man is a suspect in a case. Do you have anywhere that we can question him?"

A casino this big would have somewhere to hold people it suspected of stealing or cheating until the Las Vegas PD could arrive. Since he'd run when they'd identified themselves, Christopher was pretty sure that he could arrest Lucas and drag him back to the local FBI field office, but it would save a lot of time if he could get something out of him first.

"There's a room near the security office," one of the security guards said. "We use it to question cheats."

"We'll do this there," Christopher replied.

He followed in the security guard's wake as he led the way, keeping a firm grip on Lucas's arm while Paige tagged along behind them.

"You don't want to do this at the nearest FBI office, or a police precinct?" Paige asked.

"I want to talk to Lucas here first," Christopher said. He didn't want to give the stagehand and card dealer any time to try to get his story straight. He could see the man shaking in the wake of his dunk into the shark tank. Maybe if he was still shaken up enough, he might actually give them the truth, rather than whatever story he'd decided on to cover the murder.

They hadn't arrested him yet, and Christopher wanted to get as much information as possible before they committed to that. The moment they brought him in, he suspected that Lucas Francisco would clam up, saying nothing, and the truth was that they didn't have enough evidence yet to be sure that they would get a conviction. Yet this was a man who had access to the crime scene, who probably had the skills and interest to commit the murder, and who had run the moment the FBI arrived. It was all deeply suspicious.

They headed to the casino's small interview room, which held a table, a couple of chairs, and a camera staring down from the corner. Christopher sat Lucas on one side of the table, and waited on the other for the right moment to speak.

In part, he was waiting for Paige. Her background in psychology meant that she often came up with insights into people that Christopher didn't see. Ordinarily, Christopher loved watching her come up with those insights.

It was… difficult now, though. Christopher had noticed the way Paige had been since Quantico, standing off slightly as if worried about getting any closer. Christopher was worried about that too. It was hard to deny that he found her attractive, but he wouldn't, *couldn't* let that go anywhere. He was a married man.

He wished that he could say he was a *happily* married man, but that didn't matter when it came to this. It didn't matter that his marriage wasn't exactly the best right now, that Jennifer was good at putting on a friendly public face but that in private things were basically falling apart. At least part of it was his job, but more of it was just that neither of them was the same person they'd been when they'd married, far too young.

All that mattered was that it would be wrong to get any closer to Paige, whatever sparks of attraction he could feel between the two of them. He hadn't even asked to be partnered with her now that she was an agent. Sauer had done that. But Christopher would make the best of it. He couldn't deny that Paige was good at what she did, and that the two of them together had been able to solve cases that might otherwise have gone unsolved.

They might even have caught a killer already, after only a few hours in Vegas.

"Why did you run, Lucas?" Christopher asked, once he'd judged that the stagehand had been given enough time to worry.

"Can't I get a towel, man?" Lucas asked. "I just fell in a shark tank!"

"They were baby sharks," Christopher replied, not relenting. He repeated his question. "Why did you run, Lucas?"

"I saw two FBI agents advancing on me. Wouldn't *you* run?"

"Not if there wasn't a reason," Paige said. "If I didn't feel guilty, I wouldn't assume there was a reason to. I'd assume that they wanted to ask questions. So, what do you have to feel guilty about, Lucas?"

The stagehand didn't reply, instead looking around with a slightly panicked expression. There was definitely something there, something he was worried about. Even Christopher could see that. Was it the fact that he'd killed someone? Was it because he'd suffocated Clarissa Bale and Mylene Jacques?

"Where were you last night?" Christopher asked him.

"What? What does that have to do with anything?" Lucas countered.

"Were you at the theater where you work?" Paige asked.

"No, why would I be there?" He sounded confused, but that might just be an act.

Christopher leaned across the table. "Isn't it where you go to hook up with women you meet on the strip?"

There was a bead of sweat now on Lucas's forehead. He seemed to be starting to understand the trouble he was in.

"And it's also where a woman was found dead this morning," Paige said. Christopher got the feeling that she was trying to gauge Lucas's reaction.

"I… I heard about that," Lucas said. He seemed to scrabble for the words, his eyes darting around as if looking for a way out. "But you think I had something to do with that?"

"If not that, why did you run?" Christopher demanded. He wasn't going to let that go. There had to be a reason.

"I… I…"

The door to the holding room burst open, revealing a woman in her early thirties. She was tall and dark haired, wearing jeans and a dark blue shirt, with a badge on her belt. She did not look even remotely happy.

"Does someone want to tell me what the *hell* is going on here?" she demanded. "And exactly why someone has just barged into this casino to chase my suspect and throw him in a shark tank?"

"*Your* suspect?" Christopher said. "Who are you?"

"Detective Sanchez, Las Vegas PD. And you are?"

Christopher got his ID out. "I'm Agent Marriott; this is Agent King."

Christopher saw her hesitate for a moment or two.

"I need to speak to you outside, Agents. Now."

Christopher looked over to Paige, then stood and went with the detective. The moment he and Paige were out in the hall, the detective spoke again.

"Why exactly is the FBI messing up my case?" Detective Sanchez demanded. "Why do you have my lead suspect in custody?"

"What case?" Paige looked as confused as Christopher felt right then.

"What case?" Detective Sanchez countered. "You come in here and cause all this trouble, then you ask what case? I've been watching this guy for days. He and his crew have been taking the house for a fortune."

Christopher frowned at that. "Explain."

"After you explain what you're doing here," the detective said.

"We're here about the murder at the theater last night," Christopher explained. "The same theater where Lucas Francisco worked, and where he had after-hours access."

Christopher saw Detective Sanchez looking conflicted. It was obvious that the seriousness of the crime Christopher and Paige were investigating was stopping her from continuing to berate them about the two of them messing with her case, but it seemed just as obvious that the professional courtesy might not last long.

"I think the two of you should come with me," the detective said.

Christopher could see Paige looking over at him, obviously waiting for him to take the lead. The relationship between the two of them had changed the moment she became an agent rather than a civilian consultant, but it was clear that she was still looking for him to take charge.

When it came to the case, he could do that. It was just with everything else that he had to be careful to keep his distance. He couldn't afford to be anything more than coolly professional with her, in case it spilled into more.

"What do you want to show us?" Christopher asked, making a decision and going to follow Detective Sanchez.

She led the way along a short corridor, to what turned out to be a security room filled with screens. Those screens showed security footage from the different tables in the casino, letting the house keep a careful eye on everything that went on there. One of those screens had cameras trained on the table where Lucas had been dealing blackjack. A sports jacket sat on the back of a chair there, and Detective Sanchez moved to sit there, hitting some buttons. Judging by the coffee cups stacked up by that station, she'd been there a while.

"*This* is from ten minutes before you showed up," she said. Images came up on the screen of Lucas Francisco dealing blackjack, the cards flickering out. "*This* is why he ran from you, Agents."

"What are we looking at?" Christopher asked.

Paige seemed to be frowning slightly, though, as if she saw something Christopher didn't. "He's looking at the man on the far left of the table strangely. He's trying to disguise it, but it's obvious that the two of them know one another."

Detective Sanchez looked faintly impressed. "That's because Lucas has been feeding him good cards all morning. Dealing seconds, holding cards back. He's good; it's hard to spot, but it's there."

"He's cheating?" Christopher said. Now that he knew what he was looking for, he could see the slight inconsistencies in Lucas's hand movements as he dealt to that one player, just a slight variation in the rhythm of the deal that shouldn't have been there, a slight stumble designed to cover something else.

"I've been watching him for days, hoping to identify everyone in his crew," Detective Sanchez said. "Crews like this are often bankrolled by bigger players, so I was hoping to get them to flip. Of course, all of them will be running now that you announced to the world that the FBI is in the building."

"He could still be involved in the murder," Christopher said, wanting to remind the detective that that took priority.

"From last night? What time?"

"Around midnight," Paige supplied.

Detective Sanchez shook her head. "Then I have bad news for you. Last night, Lucas here was dealing poker to a room full of high rollers, helping one of the players there to win the better part of a million dollars. I have the video, if you want to watch it."

Christopher felt a sinking feeling as the detective said that. They'd struck out on this lead, and already used up most of the day doing it. Lucas Francisco might not be an innocent man, but the very fact that he'd been busy committing other crimes gave him the alibi he needed for the murder.

He and Paige needed to look somewhere else if they were going to find the killer, and they were running out of time. With a killer who had struck twice in a matter of days, he might kill again at any moment.

CHAPTER EIGHT

He was at a party. It was a good party, a masked costume party, and that was always more interesting than the other kind. He liked seeing the faces that people chose for themselves, because those said more about who they really were than anything that nature gave them.

Of course, it also helped that the mask he wore hid his face completely, making sure that no one would see him doing this part. No camera would give him away, no witness would be able to describe him. It was important that he was able to remain unseen while he went about his work.

Oh, they would be able to describe *some* parts. His chiseled body was encased in a suit that was deliberately dark, aside from a waistcoat that glittered with a red paisley pattern. The square line of his jaw was visible, and the piercing blue of his eyes. His dark hair was contained under a top hat, and he wore white gloves, carrying a thin wand just to complete the impression.

Currently, he'd gone for a mask that shone with elaborate, almost manic, swirls, the features built out with an alarmingly extended nose and bat-like ears. It made him look both mysterious and almost mystical, adding an almost demonic edge to his magician's ensemble.

He moved through the crowd easily, watching the people there, looking for someone perfect to help him with his next performance. He paused at a group of party-goers, made a glass of champagne disappear beneath a cloth, and then walked off with it while they were still trying to work out how the effect was performed. It was important to leave people wanting more. He sipped the champagne and then set it aside.

Everything about this party was elaborate. It was set in a vast space within one of the more exclusive clubs in the city, the walls mirrored so that it seemed bigger still. Lights above lit the place up in every color of the rainbow, while the booths at the edges were the only seating, leaving most of the place free for mingling or dancing.

Entertainers wandered through the crowd. A juggler tossed balls high, having to push through the crowd to catch them. Up on a stage, a couple of dancers in bodysuits moved in ways that switched from the elegantly balletic to the angular in a heartbeat. A hack magician in one corner performed close up magic, almost bungling a basic Hermann pass and having to cover it up by pretending to almost drop the cards he held.

Amateur.

A great magician had to create great effects, had to leave a sense of awe in the people he performed for. He had to create the sensation among his audience that what he had done was truly impossible, to suspend their disbelief so thoroughly that they experienced the effect the way they might experience true magic. There was something pure about that.

He moved through the party, performing his own effects as he went. He stopped at a table of young women celebrating an engagement, bent over to kiss the hand of the soon to be married woman, and palmed her engagement ring. He then made it appear on her soon-to-be maid of honor's hand instead. He spotted a banker there on a trip who was obviously carrying drugs, quickly pickpocketed them, and ensured that they found their way into some of the drinks.

Anything that would cause a little chaos, snap people out of their dull, ordinary lives.

He paused with a couple to perform a small mentalism routine where he guessed the unlock code for the woman's phone, easy enough with her hand on his chest, the unconscious micro-muscular movements giving him all the information he needed. Then he tossed the phone to the man, already open to the most embarrassing photograph he could find in the few seconds he had it.

His last two big effects had achieved the level of impact that he wanted. He was acquiring just the audience that he wanted. There was a buzz about the whole thing, local and even national news picking it up. There was a kind of thrill to that, knowing that he was building a following, a wider audience who would be waiting for his next performance.

Of course, that came with the pressure to produce that next performance. A small scale performer like the one working the other side of the party might be able to show off the same effects over and over, trusting that it would be the first time any of the people he was performing for had seen it.

Someone performing on a bigger stage, though, couldn't afford to repeat themselves the same way twice. Performing the same trick again to the same audience meant that they would be looking closer to find the mechanism for it. If one had to repeat the same effect, it was important to vary the method, making it that much harder to spot.

It was even better to come up with something new, and that was why it was important to find inspiration anywhere he could. For example, he had only today heard about a casino croupier who had fallen into a shark tank over at the Illustrious.

That sparked thoughts of some of the great effects of the past, Houdini's water tank escapes in particular. There was something there. It was only a question of working out the details. That was the way to produce a trick, starting with the effect, the way it should look, and only then worrying about the method.

Not that the method wasn't important. The audience should never fully understand the workings, or it took away some of the sense of mystery. In this case, mystery also meant that the police wouldn't be able to get close to him. That was important, when he still had greater effects to perform.

He kept moving through the party, and now he spotted her. The woman he'd been looking for since he got in here. The moment he saw her, there in a white half-face mask and a white dress complete with wings designed to make her look like an angel, he knew that it had to be her tonight. She was young and flame haired, slender and athletic.

He went to her, abandoning his performances for the rest of the party as he moved into the space in front of her and offered her his most winning smile beneath the mask he wore.

"Ah, an angel," he said. "Can you perform miracles?"

She looked him up and down, then returned his smile. There were definitely moments when it helped to be good looking. It meant that women ran towards him, not away. "Sometimes."

"So can I," he said, and made a coin appear in his gloved hands. He spun it over his knuckles, made it disappear and reappear in the other hand, then doubled it.

"You're one of the entertainers here?" the young woman asked, sounding surprised.

"Can I tell you a secret?" he said.

She cocked her head to one side. "Sure."

"I'm not one of them. They just think I am. Honestly, I don't even have an invitation to this party." He laughed as he said it, and she laughed along with him.

"So what are you doing here?" she asked.

"Oh, you know, causing a little trouble, having a little fun, and looking out for the most perfect woman in the room."

Her eyes widened very slightly at that. "That seems pretty ambitious."

"And yet I feel as though I've succeeded," he said, turning up the charm. "I'm Martin."

It was a fake name, but names inspired confidence and trust. He had a whole stock of them.

"Sienna," the young woman replied, and it wasn't a fake name. He knew that. "I like your mask. Although I find myself wondering about the face underneath it."

"Well, half of the fun of costumes is getting to remove them," he said. He gave Sienna a pointed look, one that said to her how much he was thinking about all the fun the two of them could have.

He was, just not in the way she was probably thinking about right then.

"I guess a magician like you could just make this one disappear," Sienna said, with a wink.

He laughed deliberately, looking her up and down. "I could certainly try."

He performed another quick coin trick, making one spin and then disappear.

"You're good with your hands," Sienna said.

"Very. Tell me, Sienna, do you know how a magician makes a beautiful woman disappear from the middle of a party?"

"I don't know," Sienna said. "How *does* a magician make a woman disappear from a party?"

He held out a hand and leaned close. "By suggesting that we could both have a lot more fun elsewhere."

She only hesitated for a moment, and he had the feeling that even that was for effect, not wanting to make this *too* easy for him. Then she took his hand.

"Sounds good to me."

He smiled as he led her from the party. He had his assistant for his next performance. Now to make it a great one.

CHAPTER NINE

Paige sat in an uncomfortable chair in the precinct of the Las Vegas PD, waiting while Detective Sanchez processed Lucas Francisco. She and Christopher had managed to borrow an office, and Paige's eyes followed him as he worked on the other side of it, going over the files there.

It was hard not to watch him while he worked, in spite of her best efforts. It was obvious that there was something wrong between the two of them, because he was barely looking Paige's way, and the atmosphere between them was awkwardly professional, where before it had been friendly and jokey.

Did he feel the same way that she did? It was hard to imagine that he could, when he was so obviously a happily married man. Paige had met his wife, and she seemed perfect. Yet he was acting the way she had before, keeping his distance as if he couldn't trust himself to be any closer.

Paige had to distract herself from those thoughts, and the best way to do that was to go back to the case files for the investigation, trying to lose herself in the details and the hunt for information. She found herself looking over the crime scene photographs again, trying to find anything that the police on the scene might have missed. She went through the evidence lists, looking for anything that had been noted too casually that might be relevant, anything that might point her in a new direction that the police hadn't considered so far.

The police looked like they'd done a good job, though. They'd been thorough when it came to the scenes of the murder, making notes of every scrap of evidence, testing everything for the possibility of DNA or fingerprints. The killer had been more careful than that, though. He hadn't left any obvious physical traces that could be used to find him.

Paige felt certain that wasn't the way they were going to catch him. If it were that straightforward, the Las Vegas PD would have done it by now. No, she needed to get back to the question of motive, and trying to understand the killer. His methods made his obsession with magic obvious. There had to be something that they could latch onto with that, something that they could use in order to get to whoever was doing this.

A killer who used magic as part of his MO. Why did that thought pull at the edges of Paige's mind? Obviously, the whole of this case was about it, but there was something else, something that Paige half remembered from her wider research for her Ph.D. Something in the past, well before this current spree.

She went looking for it on her computer, typing in the words "magician serial killer" into her search engine. Inevitably, the most recent results were all news or comments relating to the most recent murders. It meant having to trawl deeper, past all of that, putting in filters specifically to exclude anything too recent and allowing her to look for older material.

Soon, Paige found what she was looking for, and it made her simply stare at the screen for several seconds.

"Christopher, listen to this. There was a killer thirty years ago in Las Vegas, by the name of Ruben Wendel, another magician. He used to specialize in making his victims vanish."

"You think this could be linked to him?" Christopher asked. "He's resurfaced, or a copycat?"

"I don't know," Paige admitted. "He can't be involved in this directly, when he's currently thirty years into a life sentence. Mostly, I just think that, if we're chasing a magician who kills, then one way to get insights might be to talk to another one."

Christopher nodded. "That might get us something. You're planning to go see him?"

"I think it might help."

"I want to keep going working through the crime scene reports and running down everyone linked to the theater. Meet me back here after you've done it?"

He wasn't going with her? Paige swallowed with sudden nerves at that thought, and had to remind herself that she'd talked to plenty of killers in the past, and that splitting up was probably the best way for them to cover the most ground at once. In any case, Paige was an FBI agent now. She should be able to do this without Christopher there to hold her hand.

It might even make things simpler if she wasn't spending all her time glancing over at him to check on him; but at the same time, could she really do this alone? She had to try.

"I'll let you know what I find out."

Paige sat in a room of the Nevada State penitentiary, really wishing at this point that Christopher were there with her. She tried to tell herself that she was more than capable of doing this alone now that she was an agent, that she *had* done this kind of thing alone in the past, but it didn't make a lot of difference to her then. In spite of her thoughts about getting away from him for a while, Paige found that she wanted him there, and not just because he was her partner. There was something comforting about his presence, something that made her feel safe.

Paige *didn't* feel safe here, not in a gray walled room, sitting at a metal table, where a metal chair opposite her had hooks to fasten shackles and a single camera stared down at her. Those measures should have felt as though they protected her from the possibility of harm, but instead, they mostly served to remind Paige of the dangerous man she was about to meet.

Paige tried to remind herself as she sat there that she wasn't just a frightened academic now, waiting in a mental institution to speak to serial killers, the way she had been before. She was a trained FBI agent, more than capable of defending herself. Telling herself that didn't make sitting here waiting for a serial killer any less creepy, though.

The door to the interview room opened and Ruben Wendel came in, flanked by a pair of guards. He was a black man in his sixties, stooped and spindly, with long fingered hands and gray hair. His wrists and ankles were contained by manacles, which the guards fastened to the table before stepping back outside.

"We'll be right out here if he gives you any trouble, Agent," one of them said as the two of them left.

Paige nodded, wanting to try to convey that she was sure she would be fine, and that she could handle anything this man threw at her. First, though, she would need to find a way to convince herself of that.

"You're scared of me," Ruben said, fixing Paige with a cold expression. There was a familiar note there, or rather, a familiar absence where something else should have been. The absence of warmth or genuine feeling. This was the all too familiar look of a psychopath who wasn't making the effort to even pretend to be normal.

"Do you *want* people to be scared of you, Ruben?" Paige asked. "I had time to read your files while I waited for you. It strikes me that fear wasn't what you were looking for when you killed."

Ruben snorted then. "And what do you think you know about me, lady?"

"I know that you *could* have killed a bunch of different ways," Paige said. "But you went for something that would draw attention. People just disappearing like magic? That made the police think from the start that it was more than just the kind of normal murders that might happen in the big city."

"Are you here to tell me all the ways I went wrong?" Ruben asked her. "Or maybe you're here because you want to reform me."

"No, I'm here to talk about other magicians who kill." Paige let those words settle in.

"What, you think I'm going to help you?" Ruben made it sound as though she'd insulted him just with the suggestion.

"Yes," Paige said. "I think you will."

"And why would I do that?" Ruben asked. That was always the tricky part with a serial killer. They didn't do things just out of altruism, because most of them couldn't even understand the concept. They often didn't want the same things as most people, either. Paige needed something very convincing if she was going to get one to talk.

Thankfully, in this case, she was fairly sure that she had something that might work.

"Because I'm the one thing you want," Paige said. She spread her hands, gesturing to herself. "An audience. That's what you've always wanted, isn't it Ruben? My guess is that most of the people here don't appreciate you, or what you did. They certainly don't let you perform your tricks."

"Effects," Ruben snapped, in a much sharper tone. "Not tricks. Only amateurs call them tricks."

Paige offered him a smile. "You see, you're teaching me something already."

Her best shot was to play up to him, to let him talk. This was a man who had killed people he thought were ignoring him; it was obvious that attention was the main thing he wanted. Giving him that might be enough to get Paige everything *she* wanted in return.

"What do you want to know?" Ruben asked. "It isn't like all of us killers are in a big club somewhere. I can't tell you who this guy is you're looking for."

"No, but you can tell me something about the way he thinks, and the way he needs to work," Paige said. "Tell me about your kills, Ruben. How did you pick out your victims?"

"That was easy," he said. "I just looked for bitches who ignored me, or who tried to condescend to me."

He gave her a hard look as he said it, making it clear that he thought she fit into the latter category.

"Am I condescending to you?" Paige asked. "I want to hear what you have to say. You know more than me about all of this, Ruben."

"Of course I know more than you," Ruben said. "Magic was my life for years. Do you know that they don't even let me have a deck of cards here? Say I start too many fights because everyone thinks I'm cheating."

"*Are* you cheating?" Paige asked, because there was something about the way Ruben said it that made her think he wanted her to ask it.

"Of course I'm cheating. Why should I play fair with idiots? Are *you* an idiot, little miss FBI?"

"You tell me," Paige said.

"I think you might be," Ruben said.

"What makes you think that?" Paige sat there, waiting.

"Two things. First, you're here talking to me, rather than out looking for how this guy is working his effects. Every magician has props, and props tend to be custom made, or bought in very specialized places. If you really had a clue about all of this, you'd be there, not talking to me."

Paige found herself making a mental note of that. The prop safe, in particular, should be easy to trace. If it had been bought recently, maybe the killer would be easy to find once she started looking down that route.

"What's the second thing?" Paige asked.

"The second thing that makes me think you're stupid?" Ruben replied. "That's the fact that you came in here alone with an escapologist and you thought you'd be fine."

He held up his hands, no longer securely manacled. He must have dislocated his own thumb to break out, or found some way to pick the lock. There was no time to think about which it might be, though, because the former serial killer was already leaping across the table at Paige with the manacles held between his hands like a weapon.

Paige had a moment to feel absolute terror as the serial killer threw himself at her, but she still managed to get her hands up to block his lunge at her. Because she was still seated, the momentum of it bore them both to the ground. Ruben wasn't a big man, but he was still bigger than Paige, his weight pressing down on her as he tried to strangle her with the length of chain he now held.

Paige twisted from under him, kicking out hard to push herself away. He tried to lunge in again at her and Paige managed to fend him off with her hands and feet, kicking his legs from under him so that he went tumbling to his back.

"Can I get some help in here?" Paige called out to the guards beyond the door. Even as she did it, she moved in on Ruben, managing to block his attempt to lash out at her with the manacles and grabbing his arm. She twisted, forcing him over onto his stomach, her weight barely enough to hold him in place.

Paige heard the cell door open somewhere behind her.

"Damn it, not again!" one of the guards said as he came running forward to get a grip on Ruben.

Again? Implying that this was something that happened fairly regularly? Something that they hadn't bothered to warn her about when they'd brought him in there. Maybe they thought that the FBI agent could handle herself, or maybe they'd been half hoping that they would have to intervene, showing her up.

Paige decided not to let any of that show on her face. She stood and dusted herself off instead.

"You might be able to escape handcuffs, Ruben, but I get to walk out of here," Paige pointed out. "You don't. Some escapologist."

Now that she was sure she was safe, she was actually quite pleased that she'd come here. She knew what she needed to do next, at least.

She hurried out of the prison as quickly as she could, heading back to the car. She took out her laptop, logging in to the FBI's systems to check the files for any details they held on the manufacturer of the safe. According to the evidence report from the crime scene, it had been manufactured by the Magical Stars of Las Vegas Prop Company.

From there, Paige started to run searches, trying to find out who worked there. She was in luck, because it seemed that the company was determined to show off its makers. The site's "about us" page had short profiles for each of them, setting out their favorite magical effects and the work they'd done for people Paige assumed were famous magicians.

Paige ran those names through the FBI system, one by one, looking for anyone who stood out, anyone who had a criminal record. She was three names in when she came across a hit far too good to ignore.

Paige called Christopher at once.

"Christopher, I've got something."

"What have you found?"

Paige could hear the excitement in his voice.

"Ruben Wendel got me thinking about the place the props for the murders came from. There's a guy who works at the Magical Stars of Las Vegas prop company by the name of Zane Caister. The same company that made the safe, and looking at their site, I think they make the prop bullets, too."

"What have you found about him?" Christopher said. Paige could hear the sudden note of interest in his voice.

"He got out of prison about a year ago," Paige explained. "He served fifteen years for manslaughter, bumped down from murder."

"He killed someone, *and* he works where the props used in the murders are made?" Christopher paused for a moment. "We need to talk to this guy. Pick me up from the precinct, and we'll head straight over."

CHAPTER TEN

Paige wasn't sure that she'd ever seen anywhere quite as strange as the Magical Stars of Las Vegas workshop. It sat on a backstreet of the city, on the outskirts, well away from the strip, and from the outside, it didn't look like anything special. Just another big warehouse or machine shop, that might have stored furniture or car parts.

The moment she and Christopher stepped inside, though, it was a very different story. The small reception area was filled with magical props, with linked rings hanging above a counter, silk scarves and fake flowers arranged in displays, a whole selection of wands and canes sticking up out of an elaborate hat stand in the shape of an elephant's foot. The whole place seemed designed to amaze and overwhelm visitors with its oddness.

There were portraits and photographs around the walls, mainly of men all striking what were probably meant to be glamorous poses. Paige guessed that they were all important magicians of the past. Christopher certainly seemed to be looking at them with a certain amount of awe.

"That's Silencio," he whispered, nodding to one of the photographs. "He's pretty much single handedly revived silent magic."

"Is that rare?" Paige asked. She was quite enjoying this whole kid in a candy store side to her partner. He might be a big tough FBI agent, but here, there was something more excitable to him, something more open and vulnerable.

Paige saw him looking around at the posters, and in that moment, he might have been a kid visiting the magic store for the first time, looking over all the gadgets and the shrink wrapped books on display as if they held all the secrets he could ever want.

It was… cute, and *that* wasn't a word she'd ever thought she would use about Christopher. Handsome, yes. Attractive, yes. But cute?

Paige found that she liked it, and had to remind herself to back away and not show any of it. It was better for both of them if things stayed awkward between the two of them, because at least then nothing could ever happen between them.

"It's one of the most difficult ways of doing stage magic, because you can't hide anything with stage patter," Christopher explained.

There was a broad Perspex counter at the front of the reception area, with a young woman sitting behind it, reading a magazine that had obviously been taken from a small rack of them devoted to the Las Vegas magic scene. She wore slacks and a dark t-shirt with the name of the company across the front, and had short dark hair, with slightly too heavy makeup, as if she were always ready for a performance.

"What can I get you?" she said, gesturing to the cabinet built into the counter. There beneath the glass were decks of cards of dozens of different patterns, along with balls, cups, fancy coins, and other items Paige guessed were useful small props for the close up magician. All of it looked individually crafted to Paige's eye.

Christopher looked like he was actually scanning the contents of the case. Paige guessed that this was a hobby of his that he didn't get to indulge all that often. It meant that Paige had to be the one to fish out her ID to present to the woman at the reception desk.

"We're with the FBI," she said, trying to sound as serious and businesslike as she could.

"That doesn't stop you from buying something," the woman replied. She nodded to Christopher. "We're doing a special on cards at the moment. Two for one on some of the lines we're discontinuing."

Christopher looked momentarily tempted, but he shook his head. "We're here to talk to someone who works here. Zane Caister."

Paige saw the young woman frown slightly at the mention of that name, as if there were something about him that she didn't like.

"Why do you want to talk to *him*?" she asked.

"We can't divulge details of an ongoing investigation," Christopher replied.

Paige was more interested in the face the young woman had made at the mention of Zane's name.

"What's your name?" she asked.

"Mari," the young woman replied.

"Well, Mari, what is it that you dislike about Zane so much?" Paige asked.

"What makes you think that I dislike something about him?"

"The way you reacted to the mention of his name." That part had been reflexive and seemingly automatic, the expression instant rather than something composed. She'd replaced it with a polite but helpful look a moment later, but it had been there.

Mari rolled her eyes. "Like I don't get enough of that kind of thing from every wannabe mentalist who comes in. The number of them who try their subliminal programming bullshit to try to get me to go on a date with them… and they *all* think that they're some great psychological genius."

"Paige has a Ph.D. in criminal psychology, if that helps," Christopher said, obviously not wanting her grouped together so casually with a bunch of stage performers. "And if she says that you reacted to Zane's name, then I'm inclined to believe her."

"All right," Mari said, throwing up her hands. "What do you want to hear? That Zane creeps me out? That every time I walk past him, he looks my way, and I wonder if he's plotting the best way to kill me?"

Actually, that was exactly the kind of thing Paige wanted to hear about. She wanted to know all about Zane Caister, and whether he was still capable of killing.

"Has he ever made any comments to that effect?" Paige asked. "Has he ever said or done anything to make you uncomfortable besides the staring?"

"I don't know," Mari said. "He's just… creepy, you know? Coming and going from the workshop at all hours. Working on those little pet projects of his."

Projects that could easily include the preparation for the murders. They were both situations that had obviously required elaborate planning, so a man who came into a workshop like this after hours only added to Paige's suspicions.

"We need to talk to him," Christopher said. "Can you take us to him, please?"

"Sure, it's just this way," Mari said. "Needless to say, anything you see back there is confidential, ok?"

It took Paige a moment to realize what she meant. If this was a workshop that made props, then they would potentially be in a position to see how a lot of magic tricks worked. Spreading that information too widely would presumably damage the value of everything the company sold. It certainly wouldn't do its reputation any good.

"We're not in the habit of spreading people's confidential business information around," Christopher said.

Mari gave him a doubtful look, obviously having seen his reaction to the magic tricks there. She probably thought that he was going to try to get as much information on how different tricks were done as he could. Still, she led the way through into the workshop proper.

At least half of it was a huge warehouse for existing props. Looking around, Paige could see wooden and metal cabinets of every shape and size, along with rows of statues that might have been made of plaster or painted canvas on wood.

"You sell all this?" Paige asked, not quite believing that anyone could sell quite that many magical props.

She saw Mari shrug. "Most of it we hire out, or we store for some of the bigger acts. They have this stuff made for their tours, but they don't want to buy a warehouse of their own, so we hire out some of our space to them."

It was still bizarre, walking through it all. There were racks of what Paige assumed were prop weapons, each more elaborate than the last. There were platforms and cunning mechanisms, along with box after box. Paige saw one labelled *Modernity: Skulls,* and found herself wondering exactly what that act entailed.

The floor wasn't a standard warehouse floor, because there were old rugs covering much of the place, many of them with faded squares on them where prop cabinets had stood in the same place for too long under lights. Trunks and cabinets were stacked up on top of one another, forming piles and walls to navigate around.

This place was a maze, or maybe it was better to think of it as a kind of fun house or house of horrors. There were so many strange objects scattered around that everywhere Paige looked, she saw something unlikely: a full length model of a mummy, an Egyptian mask, a sculpture of a swan designed to look as though it was made from ice.

Paige could hear the sound of tools now, and it was only a moment or two longer before she and Christopher came out into a large workshop space. There were individual benches set out around it, each one surrounded by props to such an extent that they were almost individual workrooms, walled in by the creations of those within. Paige saw someone in one corner welding a huge buzzsaw blade onto a frame, saw another man sharpening the edge of what appeared to be a guillotine. At the other end of the scale, a man in one corner was working on an intricate device with the care of a watchmaker, and a woman was looking in a mirror, a flame appearing and disappearing in one outstretched hand while she made notes with the other about a device strapped to her wrist.

"Which one is Zane?" Christopher asked.

Mari pointed to where a man in his forties was working on a large cabinet that had been made to look like some kind of scientific, see-through pod. He was wearing blue overalls and had streaks of oil on his face. He was maybe six feet tall, broad shouldered and muscled in a way that filled out his overalls. He was kind of good looking, clean shaven and dark haired. Paige could imagine him up on stage somewhere, playing his part, getting the audience to go along with everything he said as he performed one of his effects.

"Have you got things from here?" she asked. "I need to get back to the front desk."

Paige and Christopher headed towards him, spreading out slightly so that he wouldn't have any room to run. At least the props hemming him in on three sides of the little workshop space meant that he had nowhere else to go.

He looked up as Christopher and Paige approached, looking somewhat annoyed by the sudden intrusion on his work.

"What are you, a double act? I don't have time for any more commissions."

Paige saw Christopher hold up his badge. "We're not a double act. Zane Caister? We want to talk to you about the murders of two women."

Paige saw Zane tense, then grab for a saw, holding it in front of himself as if he might use it as a weapon to fend the two of them off.

"Stay back!" he yelled, his tone angry and fearful in equal measure.

Paige had her gun out in an instant, taking up the perfect shooting stance that had been drilled into her back in the academy. She saw that Christopher had his Glock out as well. Paige could feel her heart beating faster with the thought of what might happen. She had only shot one person in her life, a serial killer who had been on the verge of killing her mother. Even then, Paige had shot to wound, not kill.

"Put the weapon down, Zane," Paige said, trying to think of a way to resolve this peacefully. "There's nowhere for you to go."

He started to back away, though, moving towards the cabinet that he'd been working on.

"Stay where you are, Zane," Christopher ordered him, his gun still leveled.

Zane threw down his weapon, but didn't stop backing away. That created a dilemma. Paige and Christopher couldn't just shoot an unarmed man. All they could do was follow, trying to get to him before he found a way to escape.

He moved into the clear glass cabinet that he'd built, and pressed a button. Smoke shot up, obscuring him as he stood there until Paige couldn't see him. Slowly, the smoke started to dissipate.

Zane Caister wasn't there anymore. He'd vanished, seemingly into thin air.

"There must be a panel in the back," Paige said, feeling the sudden fear that she and Christopher were about to lose their suspect thanks to a magic trick. That a killer was going to get away because of some false door that let him get to a secret way out.

She set off out of the small workspace, trying to get to the area behind it, but Christopher called her back.

"Paige, wait!"

Paige frowned. Their suspect was getting away and he wanted her to wait? Was this some attempt to keep her safe?

"I don't think that's how this trick works," Christopher said. "I've seen it online. There are definitely versions where you use a panel at the back, but for this one…"

He wrenched open the door to the cabinet, and started to poke around the interior. Paige saw a look of triumph cross his face, and he pulled at a section of the floor, lifting the thin metal of a trapdoor and stepping back with his gun trained on the cavity it revealed.

Zane Caister was crouched there rather pathetically, blinking up at them from the cramped space. Paige realized that if she'd gone with her instinct about the trick, she and Christopher would have gone away from the workshop space, giving Zane a clear path to escape. Only Christopher's understanding of the trick had stopped him from escaping.

While Christopher kept his gun trained on the cavity, Paige moved forward, hauling Zane from it.

"Zane Caister," she said. "You're under arrest."

CHAPTER ELEVEN

It was getting late, and all Paige could do was stand outside the interview room they'd put Zane in, down at the local police precinct, waiting for his lawyer to arrive. He'd flatly refused to say anything without one present. Was that because he knew he was guilty, or just because he'd spent long enough in the criminal justice system to know that it was better to say as little as possible?

Either way, it was frustrating to be stuck out there, not making progress, when they had a suspect in custody. Before, Paige might have spent a moment like this talking with Christopher, but now, she wasn't even sure that she could do that. There wasn't the same easy banter that there had been between them before. He seemed to be keeping his distance, as if aware of everything that Paige felt when it came to him. As if that knowledge had driven some kind of silent wedge between the two of them.

Paige found herself hoping that she hadn't somehow ruined their partnership even as it began. She'd tried not to do anything that would make how she felt about Christopher obvious, but it seemed clear that she hadn't managed it. He must have worked it out because he currently didn't seem to want anything to do with her. Why else was he keeping his distance like this?

Paige tried to focus on the case to distract from the worry of that. Ultimately, both she and Christopher were there to do a job. Lives were on the line. Compared to that, anything they might or might not feel was secondary.

Even as Paige thought it, a slight, shuffling man in a designer suit, carrying a shiny briefcase came up to the interview room. Christopher moved to intercept him, but the man held out a card, presenting it almost as if he were bestowing some great favor.

"I'm here to see my client," he said.

Christopher had to step out of the way to let him pass, and it wasn't long before he was ensconced in the interview room with Zane, obviously running through the whole situation.

Something didn't feel right to Paige about the whole situation. "Isn't it a bit odd that a man like Zane can afford a lawyer like that?"

"You have a point," Christopher said. "A guy like him, you'd guess he'd get the public defender. Looking at his file, I kind of get the impression that's why he went down for so long last time."

"He got sent away for manslaughter rather than murder," Paige pointed out. "His lawyer must have been doing *something* right. And that guy looks…"

Well, mostly he looked highly paid. He looked like the kind of lawyer that someone much richer might have had. Certainly not the kind of lawyer that a man who designed magic props for a living might be able to afford.

The lawyer came to the door of the interview room, beckoning Paige and Christopher in as if he were the one in control of the whole situation, rather than the two of them.

"Come in, and we'll get this all straightened out," he said. He made it sound like some minor misunderstanding, rather than his client being arrested on suspicion of being a serial killer. Paige suspected that nothing about this interrogation was going to go quite the way she might have expected.

Paige and Christopher went into the interrogation room, taking their seats opposite Zane Caister. He looked a lot more poised than he had been when they'd brought him in. He looked confident now, even defiant and angry, as if the presence of his lawyer had energized him.

"I'm Jeremy Liston," the lawyer said. "A partner with Liston, Barr, and associates. Would you like to tell me, agents, on what grounds you've arrested my client?"

"We went to question your client in connection with two murders," Christopher said. "He then proceeded to threaten us and to try to escape. That was more than enough to arrest him for further questioning."

"Zane, do you want to tell the FBI why you ran from them?" the lawyer said.

"It was the FBI," Zane said, with a shrug, as if that answered everything. As if anyone would have run the moment they found that out.

"What do you mean by that?" Paige asked.

"What do you think?" Zane countered. "The cops framed me for murder once."

He was claiming that he was framed?

"A jury didn't agree," Christopher said.

"Whatever miscarriage of justice there may have been fifteen years ago," the lawyer said. "The fact remains that my client has an understandable mistrust of law enforcement figures. One that constitutes a reasonable explanation for his actions, and certainly doesn't amount to an admission of guilt on his part."

Paige noted that the lawyer was talking far more than his client was. Zane projected a confident look, but she also saw the way that his eyes darted around, as if he were still looking for a way out of all of this. He was scared, and his confidence was mostly down to the presence of his lawyer.

"We're looking for a murderer who bases his crimes on magic tricks," Paige said. "Ones that have used props manufactured by your company, Zane."

Zane grunted and shrugged, not saying more than that.

"That amounts to no more than circumstantial evidence," the lawyer said. "As I'm sure you both know, agents. Are you really telling me that you arrested my client for that?"

"As I said, we *arrested* him because he threatened us and tried to escape," Christopher replied. "We went to ask him some questions because of those apparent connections. If he'd supplied us with good answers, then things wouldn't have gone any further."

"Sure they wouldn't," Zane said. "Just like last time, when the cops said that everything would be fine if I just talked to them. That they would get everything straightened out soon. And then they ensured that I got sent down for a murder I never committed. It took Jeremy here to get me out."

So that was the connection between the two, although it still raised the question of why Mr. Liston had chosen to get involved in the first place.

"What was it about Zane's case that got you involved, Mr. Liston?" Paige asked.

The lawyer raised an eyebrow at that. "I believe, in general, that questions go towards the suspect rather than their lawyers. But in this case I'll go along with it. I chose to represent Zane because my firm takes an interest in miscarriages of justice and police corruption. We are currently in the process of suing the Las Vegas PD in connection with a number of cases where officers leapt to conclusions and then pushed through convictions that saw people locked away for far too long."

He made that into a threat, the implication clear that the FBI could be added to the suit all too easily. Paige had no wish to find herself sued on her first case as a full FBI agent, but she had even less wish to be bullied into letting a criminal walk free if he was guilty.

"Your case on behalf of your client doesn't make *our* case go away," Christopher said, obviously thinking the same thing. "We're looking for someone who has been killing someone using the methods of magic tricks, and props that come from the company that your client works for."

It was no more than a restatement of evidence that the lawyer had already tried to dismiss, but maybe that was the point. Maybe it was a way of telling him that this wasn't going away just because he wanted it to.

"Did you work on airtight safes, Zane?" Paige asked. "What about prop bullets for the bullet catch trick?"

Zane glared at her, looking over to his lawyer. The lawyer nodded to him, indicating that it was ok for him to answer.

"Sometimes. We all work on whatever's needed."

"And do you have access to the warehouse when you want it?" Christopher asked.

"You're asking my client if he has a key?" Mr. Liston asked.

"I'm *asking* if he was in a position to take those props out of there, move them over to the locations of two murders, and then use them to kill two women," Christopher shot back. He obviously wasn't in a mood to let the lawyer dance around the questions on behalf of his client.

"This is just like fifteen years ago!" Zane said. "Asking me questions! Making insinuations! I didn't kill Bethan. I never laid a finger on her!"

"Bethan is the woman you were convicted of killing?" Paige asked. This might not be the murder they needed to talk about, but if they were able to get Zane talking about this, then maybe he would also be willing to talk about what was happening now. Maybe once he started talking, he wouldn't be able to stop.

"Don't pretend like you don't know all about it!" Zane snapped at her. "I know what you're all like. You learn every little thing about someone, and then you pretend like you don't know anything."

This was one rare case where Paige *didn't* know. She had read the file on Zane closely enough to know that he had a record, and to know that he'd been put away for manslaughter, but after that, she'd been caught up in the possibility that she might have found the killer. There had been no time to look deeper into him before they brought him here.

"Why don't you talk us through it?" Paige said. She wanted to find a way to bring things back to the most recent murders, but she suspected that the only way to get Zane talking was to talk about the killing he was willing to discuss.

"My client has already been through all of this with the appeals courts, and the probation board," his lawyer said. "We're continuing to go through it in litigation with the Las Vegas PD. I don't see what going through it all now achieves."

Zane seemed to be willing to talk though, at least about that aspect of the past, as if the sheer sense of indignation he had about it all made the whole thing come bubbling up out of him.

"People think I killed her because she died in the middle of a trick. It was an accident. Just an accident. I didn't even know that she was going to get in that box to run through her part."

"But you *had* just argued with her the night before," Christopher said. He'd obviously read deeper into Zane than Paige had while she'd been driving over to collect him.

"That doesn't mean anything!" Zane said. "And my prints were all over it because it was *my* prop. I never wanted her dead. I would give anything to go back there and save her in time."

He sounded as if he meant it, but that might just mean that it was a story that he'd embedded so deeply into his psyche over the preceding fifteen years that he'd come to believe it.

"And then they put me away for fifteen years. Fifteen years, when I could have been making it big," Zane said, as if that were the main point of all of this. Not the fact that a woman was dead, or that he'd been in prison, but that his magic career hadn't been what he'd hoped it would be. Was he really that obsessed by magic? "The Las Vegas PD should compensate me for every day of that."

"We're not the police," Paige said, wanting to create whatever distinction she could between them and the people he thought had wronged him. "We're the FBI."

"You think that makes things better?" Zane asked.

"Tell us about the safes that you worked on," Paige said. "Did you finish one recently? Did you deliver it to someone?"

Zane shrugged. "We sell those all the time. There are plenty of escapologists in Las Vegas."

"What about prop bullets?" Paige asked.

"If you want details of who we sell to, you need to ask at the store for our client lists. Not that they'll give them to you. It's confidential."

He was shutting them out again, refusing to talk to them, refusing to give them anything that might actually help. Paige had to hold back her frustration. It seemed, though, that Christopher wasn't going to do that much.

"Listen to me," he said. "If you don't start talking, then I have to assume that you have something to hide. Your lawyer got you out, but it's on probation, right? Forget the murder, just the fact that you brandished a weapon at two FBI agents and ran will be enough to revoke that."

"You wouldn't," Zane said, but Paige could hear the fear there in his voice.

"Not if you start talking. Where were you last night? Around midnight."

Zane glared back at Christopher, still looking like he might not say anything out of sheer spite. He looked over at his lawyer, who nodded to him, obviously encouraging him. The moment he did that, Paige felt a hint of worry. If the lawyer was that confident, what did that mean?

"I was at a showcase!" Zane said it as if it were the most demeaning thing he could have been doing. As if it were almost worse than the possibility of him being a killer. "Up on stage at the Blue Zephyr, not getting paid, and getting told that my act wasn't 'edgy' enough. They kept me waiting around for two hours, and barely gave me five minutes on stage. They mostly just wanted me there so that they could try to get me designing effects for one of their young guys."

Meaning that he had an alibi with plenty of people. People had been staring at him on stage. He simply couldn't have been there to kill Clarissa Bale.

"You really think this could be me?" he said. "You think I have time to do anything like this? I work for a living. I'm too busy producing effects for people, working on my act, trying to get noticed after fifteen years away!"

There was a force there that made Paige recoil. The words also devastated her, shredding her last hope that Zane might be the killer.

At the same time though, there was something about Zane's words that Paige latched onto. Zane said he didn't have the time to commit murder? So, who did?

CHAPTER TWELVE

Paige could feel the frustration running through her as they had to release Zane Caister.

"Thank you, Agents," his lawyer said with a smile that was obviously calculated to be as annoying as possible. "My client and I will discuss whether to add you to the suit in the morning."

So now, as well as having struck out again on the case, there was the risk of getting sued as well.

"Don't worry about it," Christopher said as Zane and his lawyer left. "Nothing will come of it. The lawyer knows that, murder or not, we might have enough to get Zane's probation revoked. He won't want to actually sue."

"That's not what I'm worried about," Paige said, although that was a part of it, and it worried her more that Christopher could see everything she was feeling so easily on her face. It made her worry about what else he might see there. "I'm worried because we just chased down what looked like our best lead, and it turned out to be a dead end."

"We'll find another lead," Christopher said. "But tomorrow. It's getting late. We should head for whatever hotel Agent Sauer has booked us into, and get started again in the morning."

Paige thought about arguing to keep going, but almost as soon as Christopher said it, she felt the wave of tiredness hitting her, hard enough that she felt like she might be about to fall asleep right there. Maybe it *would* be better to get some sleep, and then start fresh.

"Ok," Paige said. "Let's find out what kind of hotel we're stuck in here."

*

The Seven Lakes Casino and Hotel was not what Paige had been anticipating when she'd heard that her boss had booked somewhere for the two of them. It was a huge, glitzy casino on the strip, complete with the seven lakes of its name out front, in what amounted to a pretty ostentatious display in such a hot, dry state as Nevada.

This was where Sauer had booked them to stay?

As she and Christopher walked in, Paige saw gamblers moving through to the casino, apparently oblivious of the time, saw a whole clutch of Elvis impersonators, presumably there for some kind of conference or competition, saw a group of young men and women moving through the place, all drunk, all wearing "What happens in Vegas, stays in Vegas" t-shirts.

The two of them headed up to their rooms, which were opposite one another across a narrow corridor on the twelfth floor. That distance didn't seem nearly great enough.

"Goodnight, Paige," Christopher said as he opened the door to his room.

What happens in Vegas, stays in Vegas. The t-shirt slogan ran through Paige's mind. It would be so easy to take that literally, reach out for Christopher, and…

No, she couldn't. She wouldn't.

Paige had to back away, fear of the possible consequences making her stumble back from Christopher. Could she keep working like this? Could she work with a guy where every moment she spent near him burned inside her, making Paige long to be closer to him?

Paige swiped the card for her own room without even saying goodnight. She all but ran inside, putting her back against the door. She was breathing hard. It took several seconds for Paige to move deeper into the room, determined to ignore everything she felt right then.

Working alongside Christopher was proving harder than Paige could have imagined. She had to do this, had to be a part of this, and not just because of the fact that there was a killer out there somewhere who might strike again at any time. Paige also had to show Agent Sauer that she could keep up with the demands of the job, that she deserved to be a part of the BAU.

If she did that, maybe he would give her the information that she needed when it came to her father's killer. Information that simply wasn't out there in the public domain.

Paige went over to the bed and perched on the edge of it, opening up her laptop. She needed to distract herself from thoughts of Christopher, and work was the best way to do that.

It helped that Zane had given her a small moment of inspiration in with the disappointment of him turning out not to be the killer. He said that he didn't have the time to be the killer, because he was too busy working on his own act and his projects for clients.

It had been a small comment, and probably not one that had been intended to be serious, but there *was* a point behind it. The two murders that they knew of by this killer had both been elaborate. They had both presumably required considerable planning. To get an airtight safe from the company and then put it in place must have taken an effort. Just the transport would have required planning ahead of time, especially when it was just one person moving it into position.

Assuming it was. Was it possible that there was a whole team doing this? No, Paige didn't think that fit. If a serial killer hired people to help him, one of them would talk once they realized what was going on.

So one magician, working alone.

Would a working magician have enough time to do all of that? More importantly, would they be able to do it without being noticed? Surely, with the hours that it would take to set something like that up, someone would wonder where they were? They would want to know why they weren't putting the work in on their own job, or might start to think that they were planning to run off to another gig or change their act.

Was it possible that this was a magician who *wasn't* working anymore? Zane had hinted at how hard the magic scene could be in Vegas, but now Paige found herself looking for more, realizing that she didn't really know enough. She found a couple of forums dedicated to magicians in and around the Las Vegas area, and quickly found a few threads that were interesting, with titles like "Why is it so hard to get a gig?" and "Is the whole scene rigged against me?".

Paige had no idea whether that was just a couple of less skilled magicians who weren't able to get work because they weren't good enough, or if the whole process of getting gigs in Las Vegas really was that hard.

Thinking about it though, what would it be like if this were a singer or an actor in Nashville or LA? Both of those cities attracted people not just from around the country, but around the world, all looking for their big break. That meant that both of them featured stiff competition for anyone trying to make it, so talent wasn't the only, or even primary, factor determining who succeeded. They had to be in the right place at the right time, and plenty of people weren't.

Paige knew that those systems produced plenty of people who thought that they should have achieved more than they did. Some of them were even right about it. The entertainment industry left plenty of people feeling bitter and disaffected about the way that their lives had gone.

Was it possible that something similar had happened here, only the killer had decided to "prove" what a great magician he was by killing people in ways that related to magic tricks?

It would need to be more than that, though, because someone who had simply failed would be just as busy with a day job. They would need to have the knowledge of magic, but also have the time free to do this, *and* the money to pay for the props.

Maybe someone who had failed after making it big? Or someone independently wealthy who wanted to be a magician but who couldn't quite manage it? Paige started to search online for anything she could find that might fit those categories, especially for magicians whose careers had failed when they were right at their peak.

The trouble was that the end of a career didn't seem to attract as much attention as its beginning. There were plenty of posts and pages relating to magicians trying to convince the world that they were the next big thing. There were none that Paige could find announcing that someone's career had fallen apart. Magicians who did that simply weren't famous enough to make the news.

It occurred to Paige that Christopher might know of some. He obviously knew more about the world of magic than Paige did, so maybe he would have heard something about magicians who hadn't made it, who had come close and then flamed out. In any case, Paige probably owed him an apology for the abrupt way she'd failed to say goodnight. Maybe they could even talk things through.

Paige was halfway to the door before she realized just what a bad idea that would be. Going to his door, now, at night, would at best lead to a really awkward conversation in which Paige might have to admit her feelings. That would make it impossible to work together.

At worst, something might actually happen. Paige had to be honest with herself about her own strength of will if Christopher answered the door half asleep and shirtless. If something *did* happen, then Paige would forever feel like a cheat and a betrayer. It definitely wasn't the kind of thing that their partnership would be able to survive.

No, she couldn't go over there. She had to keep the space between them, for both of their sakes.

Paige went back to the bed, lying there and staring up at the ceiling. It wasn't just Christopher that she was thinking about. If anything, she suspected that the intensity of things with Christopher right now was at least partly a deflection, an attempt to think about anything other than the fact that her father's killer had resurfaced.

That was making things more difficult for her around Christopher, because Paige's emotions were all over the place right now, trying to deal with the fact that the Exsanguination Killer was still out there somewhere.

Paige couldn't stop herself from going back online, looking for details of the Exsanguination Killer. There were more stories, but as far as Paige could see, they all said the same thing as the ones yesterday: that this was another presumed kill by the serial killer, and that the FBI wasn't releasing details.

Paige swallowed as she logged onto the FBI's systems remotely. It would be so easy to type in "Exsanguination Killer" and see what came up. She would know what the FBI was up to with the case, and she might even be able to do something to help catch him. That would at least make Paige feel as though she was doing something.

Except that Paige knew perfectly well that a search like that would send up flags, and when Sauer found out that she was searching for this case, Paige would be lucky if he didn't fire her straight away. He'd told her to focus on the case in Las Vegas, and if she didn't do that… well, she might never be in a position to catch the killer.

Paige shut her computer and got out her phone instead. She called her mother, because Paige wanted to make sure that she was ok. Her mother would have seen the news, and even if her approach to life was to shut this kind of thing out, Paige was pretty sure that at least some of it had to affect her.

She went straight through to her mother's voicemail, though.

"Hey, Mom, it's me, Paige," Paige said. "I was just calling to check in with you. I wanted to make sure that you're all right. I… I'm sure you've seen the news. I'm working out in Las Vegas right now, but call me, ok?"

Paige hung up, but she still felt as though she needed to talk to someone. Paige felt twitchy, like if she didn't get some of this out, she wouldn't be able to sleep at all, and that wouldn't help her to do her job. There was only one person she could think of who would be there to take her call any hour of the day or night, and who would understand the whole mess of feelings that the latest murder by the Exsanguination Killer was throwing up.

Paige called Professor Thornton, her former Ph.D. supervisor, and the academic picked up after a few rings, in spite of the late hour.

"Hello, Paige," he said. "I was half expecting that you would call me."

"You saw the news, then?" Paige said. "That he's killed again?"

"I saw it," Professor Thornton said. "How is that making you feel right now, Paige?"

"I feel…" Paige was struggling to get her feelings into any kind of order right now, but she did her best to explain it all to the professor as best she could. "I feel like everything is out of control. I'm working a case with Christopher, down in Las Vegas."

"The serial killer who is using magic tricks?" Professor Thornton said.

"How did you know?" Paige asked, a little surprised.

"Paige," the professor pointed out. "I'm a professor of criminal psychology with an interest in such things. It's the kind of news story I pay attention to. Do you feel as though *that* is getting out of control?"

Paige wasn't sure how much she should say. She trusted the professor, obviously. She knew from experience that he wasn't going to repeat anything she said to him. Indeed, since they'd had formal therapy sessions in the past, there was a good chance it was all covered by privilege anyway. Yet still, she found herself trying to work out how to say it, because now that she was an agent, she couldn't give away too many of the details.

"We're running into dead ends," she explained, "and with each one, it's like a reminder that I never managed to find my father's killer."

"That was never your job," Professor Thornton said, in an even tone.

"It kind of is, now," Paige countered. In any case, that wasn't the point. The point was that every time she failed, it was like the pale, bloodless body of her father was staring up at her from the forest floor, disapprovingly.

"But then there's all this stuff with Christopher," Paige said, because everything seemed to be tangled up together.

"This would be Agent Marriott? Are you two working together again?"

"We are," Paige said. "And I thought that would be good, but…"

"But you find him attractive?"

Trust Prof. Thornton to cut to the heart of it like that.

"What? How did you know that?"

"I've seen you around him before, Paige," the professor pointed out. "It wasn't hard to spot, given how well I know you."

"But nothing can happen," Paige said. She had to stay determined about that. "We're partners, and he's married."

"And *has* anything happened?"

"No!" Paige was horrified by the thought of slipping over into that kind of betrayal. "Of course not. It's just… every time I look at him I remember that I shouldn't be doing anything, and that makes it hard to relax around him even for a moment. I shouldn't feel like this."

"And do feelings do what we want them to?" the professor asked, in a patient tone.

"No," Paige admitted. That part was so obvious when the professor said it. "It's just another thing I can't do anything about."

"Paige, you're being very hard on yourself," Professor Thornton said. "And frankly, a little arrogant."

"Arrogant?" Paige couldn't help the note of surprise that crept into her voice then.

"You're acting as if you ought to be in charge of everything around your life. As if you're the only one who can find the killer who killed your father, and as if you should be in perfect control of your feelings. As I understand it, your one job is to find the killer in Las Vegas."

"But I'm not exactly making headway with that," Paige said.

"How long have you been working the case?"

"A day," Paige replied, and felt a little embarrassed as she said it.

"Which is hardly any time at all," Professor Thornton pointed out. "You need to be kinder to yourself, Paige. I'm sure you have all the skills you need to work on this case, or you wouldn't be there, but you can't expect yourself to be superhuman. Do you have ideas about where to look next?"

"I had this idea about failed magicians," Paige said. "But I'm not sure how to go forward with it. And we never really looked into the client lists of the company that built the props used in the murders."

"You see, you have options," Professor Thornton said. "You can handle this, Paige. Just remember that to do it, you and Agent Marriott are going to have to work together."

CHAPTER THIRTEEN

Sienna came back to herself slowly, her head aching like it might explode at any minute, her vision fuzzy. So far, so normal when it came to some of the parties she went to in Las Vegas. Frankly, if she didn't wake up feeling like this after a party, she would have felt like she wasn't making enough of an effort there.

Sienna looked around blearily, trying to work out where she was, whose bed she was in, and how many of her own clothes she was wearing. Sienna vaguely had memories of a particularly handsome man in a mask, one who had performed magic tricks for her, but who had remained more than attractive enough to catch Sienna's interest in spite of that.

She remembered agreeing to go outside with him for some fun. Again, perfectly normal, but after that…

Sienna was coming back to herself more now, enough to recognize that she wasn't in the dress she'd gone to the party in. That kind of thing happened. That was practically normal, but she didn't usually wake up in a sequined leotard, shining silver, in a way designed to catch the light.

There *were* lights, spotlights in fact, shining down in a rainbow of colors that reflected from the sequins of the leotard.

Sienna might have worried about all that, or about the fact that someone had obviously dressed her in the leotard while she'd been asleep; but right then, all Sienna's worries, all her fears, were reserved for the fact that someone had bundled her up in ropes and chains, wrapping them around and around her, tying her until she could barely move.

Sienna had been on some wild nights with people before, but never anything like *this*. This was far too extreme, far too terrifying.

"What's going on," she called out. "where am I?"

It was hard to see much about the place she was in, thanks to the glare of the spotlights. Sienna vaguely had the sense of some larger space, where people might have been looking down at her from rows of seats, but all she could see right then was the wood of the platform on which she lay, and beyond that…

Beyond that, there was a large glass tank filled with clear, pristine water. In that water, small shapes swam around and around. It took Sienna a moment or two to realize that they were sharks: small ones, but still sharks.

Now, her fear blossomed into a deeper kind of terror, and Sienna found herself staring around the darkened space, trying to make some sense of it all.

She'd been at the party, she'd gone outside with the handsome man in the strange mask, and then… and then Sienna could remember nothing. He must have drugged her somehow, but Sienna couldn't remember the moment when it had happened. Honestly, she had bigger things to worry about than the precise moment when she'd been drugged. Those were *sharks* down there, after all.

"Help!" Sienna called out, in case anyone was listening. "Somebody help me!"

"Ladies and gentlemen!" a voice boomed, seeming to come from all sides at once. It took Sienna a second to realize that it was coming from speakers set around the space she was in. "Tonight, we have a very special act to present to you: the amazing Sienna!"

The voice sounded familiar. Sienna remembered it as belonging to the man in the mask. Martin, was it? Right then, it seemed worse that she knew his name, not better. Why would he tell her his name? Someone who told you their name wasn't someone who was planning on letting you go.

"What's going on here?" Sienna demanded. "What's this about? I never did anything to you!"

As far as she knew, she'd never even met the guy before in her life. She certainly hadn't done anything at the party that might make anyone want to do something like this to her.

There was nothing that could make someone want to do this to her, or to anyone else. Unless this was all some sick joke, some attempt to scare her. There were people who might want to do that, but even among those, who would go to the trouble of getting *sharks*?

"Talk to me!" Sienna demanded. "Tell me what's going on. This isn't funny!"

"Tonight, for your entertainment, the great Sienna will be attempting an escape from shark infested waters. She will have to escape the chains that hold her, untie the ropes, and swim through the waters surrounded by sharks to get to the key that will unlock the lid to the tank!"

"No!" Sienna called out. "What are you talking about? I'm not going to do any of that. I never agreed to any of this! You can't do this!"

With how elaborate all of this was, surely this had to be some kind of joke. There was a film crew somewhere, recording all of this for some kind of show in which Sienna was going to be humiliated. They were going to show all of the footage of her crying and begging, and she *was* crying now, tears falling down her cheeks as she looked down in terror into the shark tank.

At the bottom of it, she could see a key, oversized and obvious, gleaming there like a prize to be snatched. It shone there, visible in between the flitting, circling forms of the sharks.

A figure approached, dressed in black, the top hat silhouetted against the lights above. Sienna could make out the mask, with its twisted, elongated features.

"Ladies and gentlemen, it's time! Please give the great Sienna a round of applause!"

He pressed something on what looked like a small remote control, and the sound of an audience going wild came out of the speakers. Somehow, that sound was more terrifying than all the rest of it put together.

"Please," Sienna begged.

The masked man put a foot against her and pushed, rolling Sienna so that she felt herself teetering on the edge of the platform, and then toppling. She hung for a moment in the air, and then hit the water with a splash.

Sienna plunged down into it, trying to kick her legs in spite of the chains. She struggled and fought, holding her breath as she tried to swim back to the surface.

Even as she did so, she saw the masked man lowering a lid into place on the tank, locking it in place. There was a brief gap between that lid and the water, but even as Sienna pushed up to it, she could feel her legs getting tired.

Around her, the sharks circled.

CHAPTER FOURURTEEN

Paige got up early the next morning, heading to one of the casino's smaller restaurants for breakfast and taking her laptop with her. She wanted to get a head start on the case.

She also wanted to get into it before Christopher woke up, so that she would be able to focus on the work, rather than on him. Paige was determined to just do her job to the best of her ability, find answers, and catch the killer. When she helped to bring him in, Agent Sauer would have to give her what he knew about the Exsanguination Killer.

Paige's first surprise came as she stepped into the restaurant and found Christopher already there, working on his own computer while he ate. Paige went to join him; whatever awkwardness there was between the two of them right now, they were still partners in this, still meant to be working together to catch the killer.

"I wasn't expecting you to be awake so early," Paige said, as she grabbed coffee.

"I'm an early riser," Christopher replied. "I thought about waking you up, but I figured I could try to get some more work in on the case while you got some sleep."

That was pretty much what Paige had been hoping to do. She found herself wondering if Christopher had done it for the same reasons, or if it had been purely about wanting to make as much progress with the case as possible.

"What have you been working on?" Paige asked.

"We found Zane Caister," Christopher said, "but we never ran down the client lists from the company he worked at. I've emailed them, asking them who bought safes and bullets from them in the last couple of years. We don't have a serial number for the safe: it's a prop rather than the real thing, but maybe we'll find something."

"You're hoping that it will be rare for someone to perform both the bullet catch and the safe escape?" Paige said. It seemed plausible to her that they might be dealing with a long list.

Christopher nodded. "They're two different styles of performance. The bullet catch is what you might call classic magic, while the safe escape is escapology. They're not just two very different sets of skills;

they tend to produce different approaches in the performers. Being good at one doesn't make you good at the other."

"So, are there a lot of styles of magic?" Paige asked. Maybe it could help to narrow down something about the killer if he favored one specific skillset over another.

"There are a few big divisions," Christopher said. "Classic magic is what you could call the standard stage magic, with large props and big visual effects accompanied by typical magician's patter. Silent magic branches off from that, just focusing on the visuals, usually to music. Close up magic is the kind you perform to a small group of people, and it's difficult because they're close enough to see more of what you're doing. Card magic and street magic are both sub-specialisms of that. Then escapology and mentalism are kind of off to one side. Someone like Harry Houdini was an amazing escapologist, probably the best ever, but when people saw his attempts to do stage magic, they commented that it was kind of ordinary, and just relied on a lot of pre-prepared devices."

"Like our killer," Paige said. "You said that both of the tricks he copied are old ones, so maybe he has some kind of obsession with the history of magic?"

"That seems possible," Christopher said.

"I had another thought last night, too," Paige said. "Zane said that he wouldn't have enough time to prepare the murders because he was working on his act. I found myself wondering if maybe it was someone who failed in their magic career."

"That has possibilities," Christopher said. "And there have been famous magicians who have given up in the past."

"I just can't work out how to find someone like that," Paige said. "If their career is over, there's not likely to be much out there announcing it."

Christopher nodded. "But it might help us to focus in on someone once we have names to work with."

That was a good point. If they got the list of customers from the prop company, and one of them turned out to be a failed magician rather than someone working actively, it might help to point them towards the killer.

"What do we do while we're waiting for the company to get back to us, though?" Paige asked.

"We can keep looking for connections between the two women," Christopher said. "If we go deeper into their lives, we might be able to find something."

Paige frowned slightly because she'd already tried to find that kind of connection and failed. The two weren't friends on any kind of social media, and hadn't spent time in any of the same places.

"What kind of connection could they have?" Paige asked. "I've tried to find ones based on place or the possibility of them knowing one another socially, but it really does look as though the killer is targeting his victims randomly."

Which made things harder, because it meant that they couldn't get ahead of him, couldn't work out where he was going to be next. It meant that they didn't know where to start looking for evidence that he'd been there.

"I'm going to try asking their families for more details about them," Christopher said, taking out his phone. "It might be that there's something there that will connect them, or that will point to how the killer targeted them. You can try going deeper into their social media. Look for anyone who has a problem with them. And maybe look for any sign that they have a connection with magic."

Paige nodded. If she *could* find something like that, then it would almost certainly be the context in which the killer had found them. She set to work on her computer, calling up what the FBI techs had been able to scrape from Clarissa Bale and Mylene Jacques's online presences.

This time, Paige didn't try to use filters and searches to narrow things down. She plunged into the data, focusing on the messages sent to the two women. Most were from friends, chatting about places they were planning to go, people they were seeing. Those weren't the messages Paige was most interested in, though.

"Hello, Mr. Jacques?" Christopher said across the table as he made the first of his calls. "My name is Agent Marriott. I'm with the FBI, and I'm looking into your daughter's case. Yes sir, I understand that this is a very difficult time for you, and I'm sorry for your loss. I was hoping that I could ask you more about her. The more I understand about Mylene's life, the more chance there is of working out how the killer targeted her."

Paige was currently looking through messages from guys trying to hit on Mylene. There were a few, and Paige looked through each message thread, making notes of the names, trying to find signs of anyone who wasn't prepared to take no for an answer, anyone who didn't take being rejected well.

That was all too easy to do. There were at least four guys who called Mylene a bitch, and a couple who told her that they hoped she would die. For a certain kind of guy, that seemed to simply be the way they talked to women online. Paige made a note of the names, and then went through Clarissa Bale's messages, doing the same. There were only a couple of guys this time, but they were there, and Paige made a note of their names too. None of those names matched up.

"I understand, sir," Christopher said. "But maybe you could tell me a little about Mylene's friends, and any places she mentioned visiting?"

Paige could see Christopher making notes, obviously looking for anything that wasn't in Mylene's social media, trying to find any point of connection between her and Clarissa.

Paige was doing the same, starting to check the names she'd gotten from the messages, looking at the men's online accounts. In particular, she was looking for any sign that the accounts might be fake, fronts used by the killer. If she did find any, then maybe the FBI's techs would be able to trace the accounts back to real people. As far as Paige could tell, though, those pages had plenty of posts over a number of years. That suggested that these were real people, separate people.

It also meant that it wasn't likely that the killer was targeting his victims that way.

"One more question for you, Mr. Jacques," Christopher said. "It's going to sound a little strange, but did your daughter have any interest in or connection to stage magic? Did she ever do magic tricks, or know any magicians? No, I understand that it's an odd thing to ask. No, you don't remember anything like that?"

Paige was also looking for any sign that the two murdered women had been interested in magic. She looked online for any sign that they'd been to magic shows or had wanted to learn more about it. There was the message that had lured Clarissa Bale to her death, of course, but beyond that, Paige couldn't see anything.

"There's nothing here about magic," Paige said.

"And Mylene's father didn't think she had any interest in it," Christopher said.

"Which means that the magic angle is only relevant to the killer." That was an important distinction. It meant that this wasn't about some spat within the magical community. It wasn't about a magician who had built up grudges against the women in the course of his act. He was killing for reasons that made sense only to him.

"I still want to call Clarissa's family," Christopher said. "Maybe they will be able to tell me something."

As he made the call, Paige found herself thinking about the fact that Clarissa had been an actress. She found herself trying to track down the roles that the young woman had played, and for each one, Paige went to the sites for the small theaters, trying to work out what had been playing before her shows. Were there any cases where something she'd been in had displaced a magician, putting him out of a job?

No, and the fact that there wasn't was incredibly frustrating. It felt as though she and Christopher were working futilely, not actually achieving anything with their efforts. Certainly not finding anything that would help to catch a killer.

Christopher put down the phone. "Nothing. A few names, but none of them are on the list of people Mylene knew."

"So another dead end?" Paige said.

"That's what investigating on the ground is sometimes," Christopher said. "The last couple of cases, things happened pretty quickly, but I've worked on cases that took weeks, even months, of work."

Months? The idea of spending months trying to catch one killer was a frustrating one to Paige. She'd spent her entire adult life not being able to find the Exsanguination Killer, not being able to understand what had happened with her father's death. She wasn't sure that she could stand the possibility of not understanding what was happening here, either.

Christopher's phone rang, and Paige half expected it to be Agent Sauer, calling to berate them for having made so little progress, and for arresting Zane Caister the night before. Paige saw the sudden tension on Christopher's face, the worry and the fear.

"Yes, yes, I understand," Christopher said. "Yes, we'll be right over."

"What is it?" Paige asked as he hung up.

Christopher looked over at her, and even before he responded, Paige could guess the answer.

"There's been another murder," he said. "The serial killer has struck again."

CHAPTER FIFTEEN

They drove to what proved to be a community performance space, apparently used by an art collective for their works. It looked like it was covered in graffiti, but Paige had the feeling that might be deliberate, forming an interlocking web of art.

The Las Vegas PD were already there, the front of the performance space cordoned off with police tape. There were plenty of reporters, too, hanging around the entrance so that Paige and Christopher had to push their way through.

"Agent King! Can you tell us what's going on here?"

It caught Paige a little by surprise that they were asking *her* that. The last couple of times that she and Christopher had worked cases together, it had been him the press had hounded for answers.

Now that Paige was an agent, it seemed that she was fair game for them to try to get what they could out of her. She tried to remember how Christopher had dealt with it in the past, and kept pushing through them.

"Agent King!"

"We're not releasing any information about the case at this time," Paige said.

"Which magic trick has the killer used this time?" one of the reporters called out.

"Are you any closer to finding the killer?" another shouted.

Paige tried to push through them.

"Is it right that a federal agent should be someone who lost her own father to a serial killer?" one of them called out.

It was old news, but it still hurt, the way it had the first time a reporter had tried to use her past against her. Paige found herself freezing up, anger rising in her, ready to lash out.

Christopher was there then, making a route through the crowd of reporters. "My colleague has just told you that we have no comment! Now step out of the way!"

Paige kept moving, following in Christopher's wake and making her way to the front of the building. To Paige's surprise, Detective

Sanchez was there outside, standing with a man in his thirties wearing a cheap suit who looked like he was in charge.

Christopher looked as if he found it just as unusual as Paige felt to see the detective there. Paige assumed that if the detective spent her time chasing down cheats at the card tables, she probably didn't find many murders landing on her desk.

"Detective Sanchez," Christopher said, as the two of them walked up. "I wasn't expecting to see you here."

"If the two of you are going to walk into the middle of one of my investigations, I figure the least I can do is return the favor," Detective Sanchez said. She obviously still wasn't happy that they'd gone after Lucas Francisco, but maybe there was more to it too. Maybe she'd seen her chance to attach herself to a murder investigation and taken it. "This is Detective Renard."

This was the Las Vegas detective who had been in charge of the last crime scene, but who hadn't been there when Paige and Christopher got there, so they hadn't had a chance to meet him. In a way, that had probably been good, because it meant that the two of them could just get on with their investigation without having to deal with questions of jurisdiction, or the need to coordinate with the local cops.

"So, you're the FBI agents who have taken over my case," Detective Renard said. He didn't sound happy about that fact. "How's that investigation going, given that there's been another murder?"

"We're making progress," Christopher said.

"Are you?" Detective Renard countered. "Another young woman in my city is dead."

It was obvious that he was planning to turn this into some kind of pissing contest, which seemed in poor taste, given that someone else was dead. What was worse, Christopher seemed to rise to it.

"We've been working on this case for exactly one day," Christopher said. "Whereas you had the murder of Mylene Jacques to work on for more than a week. What did you find in that time?"

Detective Renard started to square up to Christopher. "Maybe without the FBI interfering, we'd have managed more."

Paige stepped in between the two of them. "We're here to do a job. Detective Renard, if you aren't going to *let* us do that job, maybe you shouldn't be here."

"You're going to try to throw me off my own crime scene?" Detective Renard snarled.

"Technically, since we're the ones who have been called in to deal with this serial killer, this is *our* crime scene," Christopher retorted. "If you want to stay, stay, but stop trying to get in the way of us doing our jobs."

Renard looked angry. In fact, he looked so furious that for a moment or two, Paige thought that he might lash out. Instead, he turned to Detective Sanchez.

"This case doesn't need me wasting my time when the FBI thinks it has everything under control," he growled. "*You* liaise with them. Tell me if they come up with anything, not that I'm expecting it."

He stormed off. It was Paige's first experience of local cops not being cooperative. The crime scenes she'd been at before had all been run firmly by the FBI, with no need to bring in the locals. Here, though, because the police had the case first, the FBI was working alongside them, and that should have meant trying to maintain good relations.

Instead though, it seemed that they were instantly at odds with the detective in charge of the case. Paige didn't know if it was better or not that Detective Renard had walked off. On the one hand, Paige didn't want to think that they were fighting the Las Vegas Police every step of the way. On the other, if Renard really didn't want to work with them, maybe it was better that he wasn't there.

"You two really are just making friends everywhere you go," Detective Sanchez said.

"We're here to do a job," Christopher replied. His tone was wary, but not as sharp as it had been with Detective Renard.

Sanchez obviously caught that too. "You think I'm going to go easier on you than Renard?"

"I think that you put the effort in on your investigations," Christopher said. "Renard wasn't even there at the crime scene last time, and now he's acting like we're the ones not putting in the work."

For a second or two, Sanchez looked as though she might spring to her colleague's defense, but she didn't. Instead, she shrugged.

"Renard has always been kind of an ass," she said. "What do you need?"

"We want to take a look at the crime scene first," Christopher said. "What do you know about what happened here?"

Detective Sanchez nodded and started to lead the way inside. "The victim is Sienna Niven. She worked as a dancer at a club well off the strip. The last anyone saw of her was at a party in a private club. She left with a guy."

Paige was impressed. Detective Sanchez hadn't originally been a part of this case, but it seemed as though she'd definitely done her homework on it. If anything, it seemed that she knew more about it all than Detective Renard would have.

"Are CSI teams working on the scene?" Christopher asked.

"Obviously," Sanchez replied. "Although they haven't found much at the moment. He didn't leave any convenient prints on the glass, and the sharks are making the whole thing more complicated."

"Sharks?" Paige said.

"You'd better see for yourself."

Detective Sanchez led the way into the performance space. There was a stage there, surrounded by seating in a kind of amphitheater arrangement. There were spotlights shining down on that stage, because apparently no one had thought to turn them off yet. On the stage…

Paige gasped as she saw the large glass tank, filled with tiny sharks. She saw the woman hanging there suspended in that tank, her hair floating around her, chains wrapping her body. The dead woman seemed to stare out at Paige, accusing her for not having caught the murderer earlier, before she had become a victim too.

The horror of that moment was so great that for several seconds, Paige could only stand there and stare at the tableaux set up on the stage. She tried to imagine what it must have been like for Sienna Niven in those last moments, terrified as she was about to be pushed into the water, then left to drown with sharks swimming around her. The thought of it was even worse, so that Paige had to take a deep breath to steady herself.

"The CSI teams are ready to pull her body from the tank," Detective Sanchez said.

Christopher nodded. "Do it."

"They'll be able to estimate time of death soon, although it must have been pretty late last night, because the sharks haven't done much damage to her body yet."

That was a reminder that the scene could easily have been even more horrific than it was. Paige knew, though, that Sienna Niven didn't need her to stand there paralyzed by how awful her death had been. She needed Paige to be a professional, and to find the man who had killed her. That meant finding the right questions to ask.

"Another theater," she observed. "Presumably accessed after hours?"

"There were no obvious signs of a break in," Detective Sanchez said, still reading from her notebook.

"At this stage, we think that might be because he's just that good at picking locks," Christopher put in. "He didn't have a key to the theater where Clarissa Bale was killed, but he broke in there effortlessly."

"I want to know how he finds these locations," Paige said. "He's picking places where people perform. Obviously, that fits in with the whole magic angle, and it makes me think that this is at least partly a performance for him, but how is he finding these places initially? Maybe if we look back through local security footage, he will be there casing this performance space, working out how he was going to do all of this."

She saw Christopher nod. "That's a good thought. I'll have the CSI teams forward any footage to FBI techs so that they can try to find any sign of him."

"Then there's the fact that he was able to get all of this in place quickly," Paige said. "Was the theater open yesterday?"

"In the day?" Detective Sanchez nodded. "They're hosting a performance art piece."

"Meaning that he had to get that tank, and those sharks, into place after the theater closed," Paige said. "What would that take? A specialist removal company? A truck of his own and specialist gear to move everything?"

"I'll have traffic check cameras around the area for a truck approaching the theater," Detective Sanchez said. She stared up at the tank. "This… this is a big step up from safes and bullets. Is it just me, though, or is all this far too close to what happened with Francisco?"

"It's not just you," Christopher said.

Paige nodded. The thought of it lent a whole new layer of worry to all of this. It looked like the killer was watching what she and Christopher did, because it was too much of a coincidence for it to be random that he had used a tank full of sharks so soon after their chase through the casino.

That raised one other interesting question, though, one that nagged at Paige, and made her wonder if they might finally have a way to start to crack this case.

"Where is he getting the sharks?" she asked. She put a hand against the side of the tank and the sharks whirled towards her. "Even in Las Vegas, I guess you can't just walk down to your local pet store and buy a tank full of them. Yet he managed to get his hands on some within a day. He managed to set all of this up in less than twenty-four hours.”

“Which means he was in a rush,” Christopher said. “We assumed that the other murders were carefully planned, but this one can’t have been planned so thoroughly. If he put it all together quickly, maybe he made mistakes.”

“Exactly,” Paige said. “And if we look up dealers in the area, I bet we can find the one who sold the sharks. If they have security cameras, or just keep records of transactions… we might have this guy.”

CHAPTER SIXTEEN

Paige was sitting next to a shark. Admittedly, it was just one of the baby sharks from the bigger tank, decanted into a much smaller fish tank and placed on a desk in Detective Sanchez's office, but it was still a shark.

It was there so that Paige could compare it to pictures online from the few places licensed to sell the creatures.

"This looks like one of the smaller species of reef shark," Paige said as she studied the pictures.

"Is that good or bad?" Detective Sanchez asked.

"It might help us to narrow down where they came from," Paige said. "Although there are more places than I thought there would be that sell exotic animals."

She saw Detective Sanchez shrug. "This is Las Vegas."

"So when someone calls up a store and says 'I'll have a tank full of sharks'…"

"They assume it's for a show, or some celebrity wants it for their dressing room, or… well, there are plenty of people who want that kind of thing to show off," the detective said.

Paige looked over to Christopher, to see if he was as surprised by it as she was. Las Vegas was obviously very different in some respects from D.C.

"I'm trying to track down anyone who might have transported it," he said. "My guess is that a haulage company would remember having to transport live sharks."

Paige nodded. "Any luck so far?"

"Not yet," Christopher said, "and it's a specialist job. There are only so many places that would be able to handle it without the sharks dying."

"All of them dying in transit?" Paige asked. "Or some of them dying afterwards from the stress?"

"Does the distinction matter?" Detective Sanchez asked.

Paige did her best to explain. "The killer wasn't looking for sharks to keep as pets, or to live through the run of a Las Vegas show. He just wanted them for this one moment, just needed them to survive long enough for the murder.”

“Meaning he wouldn’t have to be as careful about transporting them,” Christopher said, obviously getting it. “So he wouldn’t have to use specialist transport. My guess is that he would hire a van or use one he already owns. The fewer people involved in it, the less chance of him being caught.”

It meant that there was less chance of tracking him that way, meaning that Paige had to hope her search for the place that had sold him the sharks would pan out instead.

“As far as I can tell, there are three suppliers who stock this particular species,” Paige said. She started to make calls.

“Ok,” she said, after a minute. “Of the three places that stock small reef sharks, only one has any in and would have been able to sell them at short notice.”

“Meaning that this has to be the place,” Christopher said. “Detective Sanchez, can you keep checking things here? I think Paige and I need to go talk to the supplier. If we’re lucky, they’ll have the killer’s details on file.”

Finally, it felt to Paige like they were catching a break in this case.

*

Exotic Aquatics turned out to be a small store that fronted onto a much larger warehouse space. It reminded Paige a little of the prop manufacturer she and Christopher had visited in that respect, just one more small but useful space servicing the bigger machine of the Las Vegas entertainment industry.

As they walked in, Paige had to admit that the store space was impressive. Every wall was covered in fish tanks, the counter was another fish tank, and several more stood in the middle of the space. Each one was a different shape, as if to show off some of the possibilities that could be accommodated, no matter how outlandish the client’s needs.

As for the creatures that were in those tanks… they were a spectacular array that even most large aquariums would have been proud of. Paige saw brightly colored corals and tropical fish in every color of the rainbow. There were octopuses in one tank, shifting shape and hue as the light hit them, and a couple of lobsters in another, ambling about among the rocks.

There were larger fish too, some as big as Paige was tall, looking cramped even in the massive tanks that were set around the room. Then there were the sharks, whirling around and around in a couple of central tanks. The sharks were the same size as the one currently sitting on Detective Sanchez's desk, the same light gray with white tips to the fins.

This was definitely the place.

A woman in her early forties came up, dressed in slacks, sensible shoes, and a t-shirt that had the silhouettes of different kinds of sharks swimming across it.

"Hi," she said. "I'm Toni, can I help you to find anything?"

Paige looked across to Christopher for confirmation, and when he nodded, she took out her badge.

"I'm Agent King and this is Agent Marriott, and we need to talk to you about those sharks."

She pointed to the tank as she said it.

Paige saw Toni frown slightly. "What about them? Wait, are you the woman who called before?"

"Yes," Paige admitted. She was more interested in the way Toni was reacting. Paige thought that she saw a bead of sweat on her brow, and her eyes were darting around nervously. "What is it you're so worried about, Toni?"

"Worried? I'm not worried about anything. But you can't just come barging in here like this. I'm trying to run a business here."

"We just want to ask you some questions," Christopher said.

"What about?"

"About sharks," Paige said. "And about an order for them that would have come in yesterday."

"I'm not sure if I remember anything about that," Toni said. "Look, it might be better if you both left."

"Could you check your records?" Christopher asked. "I'm sure you keep records of everything. Especially when the purchase would only have been yesterday."

Toni started shaking her head, though. "We can't just go around handing over our records to the FBI. Some of our clients are important people. They rely on us to be discrete."

"They're buying huge fish tanks with exotic species," Christopher replied. "I'm not sure that discrete comes into it. What are you trying to hide, Toni?"

"I... this is all entrapment, or something. You can't do this, coming down here, pretending that you were a customer over the phone, trying to get me to admit to something."

"Admit to what, Toni?" Paige asked. "You've been nervous ever since Agent Marriott and I walked in here. Is there something going on here that we need to know about?"

"Or perhaps that Detective Sanchez of the Las Vegas PD needs to know about?" Christopher said.

"I don't know what you're talking about," the store owner said.

"So if I were to call her, and suggest that she come here to check every piece of paperwork you have for the import of so many exotic species..."

Paige could see that he'd hit a nerve there. Toni actually flinched. Paige wondered exactly which of the creatures there she was worried about. Maybe the sharks, maybe some of the exotic coral, maybe something even more special.

Apparently, Christopher could see it too. "Then there's the question of whether you're keeping the animals safely, and in the right conditions, and of course, I could call the IRS too, to check that you're paying everything you should in import taxes..."

The message was clear: he could make Toni's life very, very difficult if he wanted. Paige knew that was her cue to play good cop. She did her best.

"Toni, we're trying to catch a murderer. The man who bought a tank from you drowned someone in it last night. That's all we're interested in. Not your paperwork, or your tax receipts, or anything like that. Just catching the killer."

Paige saw the store owner considering. "And if I do that..."

"Then we won't have enough time to start looking into your business," Paige said. "We really do just want to catch a killer. You want to help us do that, don't you, Toni?"

"Yes, of course," the store owner said. "Of course I do."

"Then what do you remember about the order for the sharks?" Paige asked.

She saw Toni pause as she tried to remember. "It came in yesterday afternoon. An urgent order, but the guy was willing to pay extra for a rush delivery. He said it was vital to a show."

"Did he come in here?" Christopher asked, obviously hoping that the killer had walked into the store and been caught on whatever security cameras the place had.

"No, the order was placed online," Toni said.

"Do you still have details of that order?" Paige asked. "Credit card details? A delivery address?"

"I… I'll check," Toni said. She went back behind the fish tank that formed her counter, typing something into the computer that sat there. She turned the screen to face the two of them. "There, this is everything I have on the transaction. The card details are anonymized for security, but the name is there, and the address."

Paige felt a surge of hope. A name and address? It was more than she could have imagined when they came here.

"If we run that…" Paige began, but Christopher was already shaking his head.

"The name is a fake," Christopher said. "John Maskelyne was a Victorian magician known for inventing a version of the levitation trick magicians use today."

The name wasn't the important part, though. The part that mattered was the address. The killer would have had to take receipt of the tank somewhere before he moved it on to the community performance space. Maybe his home, maybe a workshop that he used for his props. If they were lucky, he would be there now, and even if he wasn't, then there would still probably be more than enough evidence there to work out exactly who they were dealing with.

"Call Sanchez," Christopher said. "Have her send some backup to that address. A guy like this could be dangerous on his own ground."

Paige nodded getting out her phone as she and Christopher headed for the exit. There wasn't any time to lose. They needed to get to the address they'd gotten out of the store owner, and track down the killer before he had a chance to strike again.

CHAPTER SEVENTEEN

He worked on the saw, sharpening it slowly, wanting it to be perfect for his next effect. He checked every tooth of it, making sure that it was straight and rust free, working on it with a sharpening stone, then oiling it carefully.

When he was sure that it was sharp, he went over to the box set on a trestle table in the old workshop that had belonged to his father, setting the saw into the groove reserved for it. He wanted to practice his stroke with the saw before the final effect of his act, the climax that would bring the attention of the world to his work.

Not that the box was his. It had been his father's just as so much of the rest of this had been. His father, who had fancied himself to be the greatest magician since Robert Houdan, who had tried everything from large illusions to mentalism, and who had sunk all of his efforts and attention into the quest to become better known and better loved.

He certainly hadn't had any attention left to spare for his son. When his father's attention *had* come his way, it had been to try to force him to assist with the magic act, then to criticize him for not doing well enough.

He sawed at the box then, anger lending a strength to the strokes of the saw that hadn't been there before.

He tried to remind himself of just how well his last few effects had gone. His audience of police and FBI agents seemed rapt in the attention that they gave to his work, and they still hadn't deciphered the mysteries behind it of who or why. Perhaps, once this final piece was performed, he would stand up and take a bow.

Or not. A magician never revealed his secrets, after all, and keeping some mystery meant that there was more chance of a return tour at a future date. A chance to work on some new ideas before he revealed them to his adoring public.

He was getting ahead of himself, though. For now, he had to focus on this last great trick. He wanted this climax to be spectacular.

He had reworked this method, of course. His father's box for sawing someone in half had been carefully designed to allow them to drop out of the way of the saw, and then to allow the two halves to be pulled apart neatly, with no danger to anyone.

It had taken him quite some time to modify this original box to be… well, just a box again. One that would hold his target very firmly in place while he set to work with the saw.

He'd had *this* effect in his mind before he'd killed any of the others. From the very start of it all, *this* was the moment that he'd been building up to. That had been another thing he'd learned from his father: that a magician planned the end to his act from the very beginning, and built towards it carefully, step by step, slowly raising the intensity.

There were probably some who might say that sawing someone in half wasn't as spectacular as drowning them in a tank filled with sharks. The sharks had certainly taken more effort logistically. Yet this final effect was far more meaningful to him, far more personal. This was the trick that his father had made him work on obsessively. The one that he'd always made the climax of his act.

Now, though, he needed to find the perfect assistant for his performance. Those for his previous ones had been more than adequate substitutes, but for this one, only one person would do.

So he called her.

"Antoinette, it's me," he said. "Sorry to call you out of the blue like this."

He pictured her as he called, so tall and slender, with that dancer's body that had kept his father so enthralled and meant that she'd never had to do any of the hard work around the act. She'd never been the one berated for getting something wrong, or made to pack away the whole act because his father was in a furious mood after another terrible gig.

He kept sawing idly as he thought about her, imagining her there with each stroke, imagining both the screams and the satisfaction of it.

"Wow," she said. "I wasn't expecting you to call like this. I don't think I've heard from you since your father passed. Not since the funeral."

That was true, because he'd been careful to have nothing to do with her, or with any of his father's old life. He'd left everything in storage, hadn't even gone to touch it, despite the part of him that had wanted to burn it all to the ground.

He'd walked away from it all, left it behind. And then… then he'd found that he couldn't. He'd found that there were some things that were impossible to move on from. He'd gone into the workshop, looked around, and *known* what he had to do.

"I had to take the time to get my head straight," he said.

"I understand," Antoinette replied. "It took me a long time to get over the loss of your father too."

As if she'd ever understood anything about him. As if she'd done anything but tease and torment him, this woman who'd been his father's assistant, his muse, and his lover.

"What's that noise?" Antoinette asked.

"Oh, nothing," he replied, stopping sawing for the moment. "Something I'm working on. Something I'd love to show you, actually. Look, you're still in Las Vegas, right?"

He knew that she was, but he didn't want to make it obvious that he'd been stalking her, looking through every facet of her life to plan how this would go.

"Yes, still in the old house."

His father's old house. He'd left it to her, while he'd only gotten the workshop.

"Would you like to meet up? I'd love to see you again, and maybe talk about Dad. It's been so long."

"I'd like that too," she said. "Tonight?"

He smiled, looking down at the length of the saw. "Tonight would be perfect."

CHAPTER EIGHTEEN

Paige could feel her heart beating faster in her chest as she sat a little way from the address that the shark tank had been delivered to. It was a large industrial space, a warehouse with corrugated iron roofing and big roller doors, exactly the kind of place that a magician might use to store his props.

It was obviously quite dilapidated, as if someone hadn't bothered with maintaining it for a few years. Paige spotted a broken window on one side, and some cracked brickwork. There were patches of graffiti that hadn't been cleared away, too, so that the whole place had the air of somewhere almost abandoned. Maybe, if this belonged to a magician whose career had stalled, he'd stopped being able to pay for the repairs.

The very emptiness of the location only increased Paige's nerves. This seemed like exactly the kind of location the killer might pick to hide out. If he was in there, then this could get very violent, very quickly.

"You could wait here and watch for anyone trying to run," Christopher suggested from his spot in the driver's seat. He could obviously sense some of Paige's worries about all of this, but even so, he should have known better than to ask.

"I'm an agent now," Paige pointed out. "I can't just sit out the dangerous parts."

She saw Christopher smile. "As I recall, I couldn't get you to do that even when you were just a civilian consultant."

"So why would I wait in the car now?" Paige asked.

"True. We'll need to stick together and move quickly once we're in there. In a space like that, once he hears us coming, he'll probably try to run or hide."

Paige was more worried about a couple of cameras she could see at the side of the building. It seemed that their killer was taking his security measures seriously, and those cameras might give him a chance to see them coming well before they could get close to him.

"We'll need to move quickly," Christopher said. "I got a warrant based on the address we got from the store, so we're covered there.

There's a side door I think I can get us through. Once we're inside, we'll need to sweep the building for any sign of the killer."

Paige nodded. This was the side of Christopher that she wasn't sure that she would ever be able to match, even though she was an agent now. It was the side that was all action, ready to take down bad guys at a moment's notice.

"So, do we go now?" Paige asked.

"In a minute," Christopher said.

He got out of the car and Paige followed as he went around to the trunk. He opened it, revealing the stash of tactical gear that the local field office had left there for the two of them. Paige strapped on a tactical vest, watching as Christopher did the same. He tossed her a shotgun, a Remington like the one Paige had trained with back in the academy. The reflexes drilled into her in that training came back to her and she checked the weapon carefully, loading it.

"Do you think I'll need this?" she asked. Her handgun was still strapped to her, after all.

"This guy has murdered three people," Christopher replied. "Better not to take any chances."

Paige nodded. Christopher had a point.

"Ok," he said. "Now we're ready. Just follow my lead in there, Paige. You'll be fine."

He said it in a businesslike tone, but Paige thought she could hear a hint of worry there. Even now, he was anxious about leading her into a dangerous situation.

"Should we call for backup?" Paige asked.

"I've texted Sanchez, but I want to move now. The longer we wait, the more chance there is of him spotting us and disappearing. I think the two of us can take one killer."

Paige hoped that he was right.

She followed as he led the way towards the building. There was a side door there, and they paused while Christopher took out a set of lock picks, working on the lock. It sprang open in under a minute, and Christopher led the way inside, gun out, ready for trouble.

Paige followed in his wake, trying to remember her training. She had to cover the angles, making sure that she dipped her weapon every time her line of fire crossed where Christopher was. She had to watch for danger, and still make progress through the building, clearing each room they passed as they went.

There were several such rooms, each one set up with a table and a few chairs, more like a series of office conference rooms than anywhere someone might have lived. There were more rooms that looked as if they might be for storage, each one locked with a padlock. If they caught the killer here, those would need to be cut off so they could search the storage lockers for evidence.

The place was well lit, at least, strip lights guiding their way along a broad corridor leading to a set of double doors. Paige stood on one side of them, her back pressed to the wall as she waited for Christopher to open them.

They moved through quickly into a much larger space, stacked with boxes, shelves, and even a couple of shipping containers. Had the killer just taken over a storage facility, using it as a place to keep his macabre props until he needed them to kill someone? Paige couldn't guess at the contents of most of the crates, and there wasn't enough time to start opening them up to look. They had to focus on catching the killer.

There was a loading bay towards the front of the place. A truck was there, and Paige could see its driver unloading a large box. Was it due to be used in the killer's next trick? Another man stood waiting, looking on with an eagerness that made Paige wonder exactly what was in the box.

This had to be the killer, and the thought of that made Paige pause for a moment, staring at him as if she might be able to see that side of him just by looking at him. It also meant that she would be able to recognize him if he ran, and pick him out of a crowd. He was a man in his thirties, tall and dark haired, good looking in his way and dressed in clothes that were casual but looked expensive. He was wearing dark slacks and a black turtleneck sweater that made him look like he wanted to be able to creep around without being seen.

She and Christopher approached carefully, moving between the boxes, trying to stay out of sight. It was important to get as close as possible before making their move, so that the killer would have fewer opportunities to get away.

Paige tried to assess the situation in line with her training. There were two big concerns for her right then: one was the open door to the loading bay, which might allow their suspect an easy avenue of escape. The other was the fact that the delivery driver was so close to him, which might allow the killer to take him as a hostage.

Both of those problems were most easily dealt with just by waiting, and Christopher made it clear that he felt the same way, putting a hand on Paige's arm and gesturing for her to crouch behind a box not far from the loading area. That moment of contact was pretty much the first time the two of them had touched in days. They'd both been so careful to keep their distance that Paige was almost painfully aware of the contact now.

She couldn't think about that, though. She had to focus on what she and Christopher were there to do. That meant crouching there while their suspect signed for the package, then waiting for the delivery driver to return to his truck.

As he did so, though, their suspect started to move away from the package. That was when Paige realized the downside of the plan: if they waited too long, then there was a chance that he might leave, or move to an area where the two of them couldn't contain the situation as easily. Paige looked across to Christopher.

He paused for a moment, then nodded and stood from behind the box with his weapon leveled.

"FBI! Keep your hands where I can see them!"

Paige joined him with her shotgun raised, ready for any sudden moves from their suspect. He was standing there looking shocked and terrified, but that just seemed like a normal reaction when someone had two guns pointed at them.

"Cuff him, Paige," Christopher instructed, keeping his gun trained on the man who had received the package.

Paige nodded, and then moved around the man, taking out her cuffs. "Put your hands behind your back."

"What's going on?" he demanded, as Paige cuffed him. "What is all this?"

"We know who you are," Christopher said. "We know this is where you had the fish tank for your last murder delivered."

"Murder? I don't know anything about any murder! I just came here to pick up a package."

"Then explain why this is the address that a prop used in a murder was delivered to," Christopher said.

The man still looked slightly panicked, but now also looked indignant. "Because that's what this place is *for*!"

"What's going on here?"

A uniformed security guard came in from the other side of the storage space, his hand on his gun. Paige saw Christopher hold up his badge.

"FBI," he said. "Who are you?"

"I work here," the guard said. "What are you doing here? Did someone order something illegal again?"

Paige was confused now, not quite sure what was going on.

"Sorry," she said. "You work here? What is this place, exactly?"

She'd assumed that it was a storage facility that had been taken over by the killer to store his props. Now, a second possibility came to her, one that, if true, would probably be deeply embarrassing for both her and Christopher.

"This is a storage facility," the guard said. "We let online sellers meet up here to take possession of goods they don't want in their houses right away, or that they're going to put into storage. We have some conference rooms too, and workspaces for small businesses."

Meaning that there suddenly wasn't the link that Paige and Christopher had assumed there would be to the killer. Meaning that the man in front of them wasn't their guy, but was instead just a random individual there to collect something he couldn't receive at home.

Paige uncuffed him.

"We're very sorry, sir," Christopher said to the man they'd leapt out on. "We thought you were someone else."

Paige knew how awkward a moment like this could be. It was the kind of thing that could generate bad feelings towards the bureau, and maybe even lawsuits. It was also an incredibly frustrating moment, because in a matter of minutes, she and Christopher had gone from being certain they were about to catch their guy to realizing that he was just one more anonymous face in a crowd of people visiting the facility.

No, not anonymous. A thread of hope rose in Paige as she thought of the cameras covering the doors. As she looked around, she saw a couple more in here, obviously meant to keep an eye on the facility's clients as they went about their business.

"Do you have access to the footage from those cameras?" Paige asked the guard.

"Yes ma'am."

"We need to see it right away."

CHAPTER NINETEEN

Paige sat in Detective Sanchez's office, reviewing the camera footage while the detective paced in obvious frustration.

"I can't believe you two didn't tell me where you were going. I could have told you that it was a storage facility that online sellers use."

"It doesn't exactly advertise that fact from the outside," Christopher replied.

"It doesn't need to, except online," the detective said. "Frankly, I think the whole place is a little shady. We've caught people meeting up to deal drugs there a couple of times before."

"Well, now you have an excuse to look closer at the place if you want to," Christopher said. He was obviously trying to sell it to the detective as a win, rather than as an embarrassment for all of them.

"You do get how this makes me look?" Sanchez said. "Since Renard dumped you on me, the department thinks that I'm basically your liaison. So when you mess up and try to arrest some innocent passerby with guns blazing…"

"They weren't blazing," Christopher said. "No shots were fired, and we didn't formally arrest anyone. Plus, we had plenty of grounds for being there."

Paige tried to focus on the footage she'd gotten from the guard. It was grainy and low quality, obviously installed as cheaply as possible. The facility's owners clearly thought that the deterrent effect of the cameras being present counted for more than whatever they saw.

"Look," Christopher said. "I need to make some calls. I have to get in touch with Sienna Niven's family, to see if they can tell us anything that might point us in the right direction."

Paige heard Detective Sanchez sigh. "I'll keep trying to run down the vehicle that brought the shark tank to the arts center. If we can find footage of it, it might give us our killer."

Which left Paige trying to find a glimpse of the killer on the security footage from the storage facility.

"Hello, Mrs. Niven? This is Agent Marriott of the FBI. I'm calling about your daughter, Sienna. Yes, ma'am, I understand how difficult it must be for you at this time. I'm sorry for your loss."

While Christopher spoke to Sienna's mother, Paige scanned the footage carefully. It helped that she knew the timeframe to look at, because she knew that the tank must have been delivered sometime yesterday.

"I just wanted to talk to you more about your daughter's life. Can you think of anyone who wanted to hurt her? Anyone who had made threats against her?"

Christopher seemed so by the book to Paige in moments like this. They'd already established that this was a serial killer, so the motives involved only had to make sense to him. There didn't have to be anything in the victims' lives that tied them to him.

"Yes I understand," Christopher said. "Well, what about the people she knew, or her job? Can you tell me more about them?"

Paige realized that she didn't have to scroll through a whole day's worth of camera footage. She had a copy of the order form for the shark tank, and that gave the time that it had been ordered. Better yet, there was a delivery confirmation attached to it, which gave the time that the driver said that they had completed their delivery.

"Her sister? Yes, of course," Christopher said. "Can you give me a number for Harriet, Mrs. Niven? Thank you so much. If you think of anything else, please don't hesitate to call me."

He hung up.

"Nothing from the mother?" Paige said, slowly scrolling through the footage to find a point maybe half an hour before the delivery time.

"I got the feeling that she didn't want to know much about her daughter's job, or who she hung out with," Christopher said. "Dancing in a club wasn't respectable enough. But she said that Sienna's sister might know more."

"There might not be anything to find," Paige pointed out. "We didn't find any connections between the first two victims."

"The killer has to have met them somewhere," Christopher countered. He went to make his second phone call.

While he did, Paige worked through the camera footage, looking for signs of the killer. She looked for the moment when the delivery had arrived first, because that would be the moment when the killer would have to be there in frame on the loading dock to receive his package.

Paige found the moment, the shark tank suddenly appearing there in fast forward, then a figure coming to it to move it with a small forklift.

Paige backed up slightly, then let the footage start to play out at normal speed.

"Hello," Christopher said as he made his call. "Is that Harriet Niven? My name is Agent Marriott, with the FBI. I need to talk to you about your sister. Your mother suggested that I might be able to talk to you to learn more about who Sienna's friends were, and about her job."

Paige found the moment when the killer started to come into shot. Her heart pounded with the possibility that she might be about to get a good look at him for the first time, and that she might have an image she could forward to the FBI's techs to run through facial recognition software.

Even as he came onto the screen, though, Paige felt her hopes ebb a little. The man obviously knew that the camera was there, and he was doing his best to make sure that the camera never got a clear view of his face. He was wearing a hat and dark glasses, with a scarf pulled up over his nose and mouth, determined not to give away the least hint of his identity. The best Paige could do was to follow him with the camera footage, looking for the moment when whatever vehicle he loaded the tank into left the storage facility.

"Did anyone ever threaten her?" Christopher asked. "Really? Who?"

That caught Paige's interest, but she tried to focus on her own job here. She wanted to find what she could from the camera footage. She switched to footage that covered the parking lot for the storage facility, focusing on the time just after the fish tank was handed over.

Paige saw the delivery truck leave, the logo for Exotic Aquatics emblazoned on the side. That wasn't the vehicle she was looking for though. *That* came out of there about ten minutes later: a gray van, with no distinguishing features. The footage was grainy, but Paige went back and forth working through it until she found…

"Yes! I have a license plate for the killer's van," Paige said.

Christopher was still making notes intently on the end of the phone, so Paige went to run the license plate without waiting for him. Maybe once she could put a name down in front of him, he'd forget about trying to track a serial killer by looking at the crime like a normal murder.

There was only one problem with that approach: when Paige ran the plate, it came back as the license plate for a Toyota Prius, not a van. The killer had cloned the license plate to avoid being tracked.

It meant that Paige had hit a dead end. Oh, maybe it would be possible to trace the van using traffic camera footage from around the storage facility, but Paige doubted it. A man careful enough to use a fake license plate would be careful enough to use a few back streets to avoid cameras on his way back. They'd had what looked like a good lead, but now it seemed that they'd lost him.

"I've got nothing," Paige said as Christopher hung up the phone. "I have clear shots of both the killer and his vehicle, but he's disguised, and his van is using a fake license plate. Maybe we can get something from traffic cameras, but I doubt it."

Paige felt almost guilty, giving Christopher that news. Even though it wasn't her fault that the killer had been careful, it still felt like it a little. It still felt as if she should have found a way to do more to uncover his identity in spite of the precautions that he'd taken.

"It was always likely that he'd be careful," Christopher said, "but I think I have something. Sienna's sister told me that while she was working as a dancer at a club, she had a problem with a guy who was stalking her. He came to see her there at the club, and then he started to stalk her online as well, hitting on her. He offered to pay her for sex, and when she turned him down… well."

He turned his phone to Paige. There was a message there, screen-grabbed from an account.

I'll kill you, bitch. No one says no to me. Especially not some cheap stripper who thinks she's too good to follow through.

"And we know who the message is from?" Paige asked.

"A guy called Mark Zint," Christopher said.

Paige tried to think it through. It was definitely a promising lead, but she wanted to make sure that it worked before the two of them started chasing after it.

"This guy, Zint, wouldn't Sienna have known his face? Why would she have gone with him last night if she knew it was him?"

"Because the party she attended last night was a masked costume party," Christopher said. "If Zint was careful, she would never have known it was him."

And they knew from the footage that the killer was *very* careful. A man like that might have disguised his voice, changed his mannerisms… it was plausible that it could have been him.

Paige looked up Mark Zint in the police database and found that he had a couple of civil lawsuits against him for sexual harassment. This clearly wasn't the first time that he'd behaved that way with women.

She searched for him online, trying to learn more about him generally, and when she did, she stopped dead.

Las Vegas magician drops out of the limelight out of sexual harassment claims, one article read. *Successful Vegas magician Mark Zint has canceled his shows and parted ways with his agent after a string of allegations against him by multiple women, who all claimed that he used stage hypnosis sessions to seek inappropriate relationships. The magician has issued a statement saying that he vehemently denies all of the allegations, and that he will be seeking treatment for depression and addiction issues.*

Paige looked over to Christopher, barely able to believe what she was reading. "He's a magician. Apparently a pretty successful one, so he has the money to do all of this. More than that, he's a magician who doesn't have a career anymore, which means that he has the time to come up with it. And it seems clear that he has some pretty obvious problems with women."

"Does he fit the profile of the killer?" Christopher asked.

Paige paused for a moment or two, wanting to be certain. There wasn't any doubt, though. As far as she was concerned, everything about Mark Zint looked like their killer.

She nodded. "I think it might be him. At the very least, he's a serious suspect."

Christopher looked pleased about the confirmation. "We'll need to tread a little carefully, though, after today. Sauer won't like it if he gets too many calls about us accusing innocent people."

"Does that mean we can't go after him?" Paige asked.

"It means that we *talk* to him. We try to find out more. And then if he doesn't give us good answers... *then* we can think about arresting him."

CHAPTER TWENTY

Paige had to admit, she hadn't realized that there was quite so much money in magic. She could only stare at Mark Zint's Las Vegas mansion with a kind of awe as she and Christopher pulled up in front of it. It looked as if someone had seen the Palace of Versailles and told the architect to recreate it on a scale that would fit in the city.

The cars outside were just as expensive. Paige saw a Maserati and a Ferrari, along with a number of other sleek black cars. Too many, she thought, for one man, although maybe Mark Zint just kept a collection of them so that he could pick one according to his mood.

"Looks like Mr. Zint has guests," Christopher said.

"Do we come back later?" Paige asked. Trying to question someone while they had people there sounded like a recipe for conflict.

"Not when we have a killer who has murdered so many people in a short time," Christopher said. "If we waste any time now, we might lose the chance to stop him before he kills again."

Paige nodded. That made sense, but she suspected that it wouldn't make any of this easy.

"How does a magician make *this* much money?" Paige asked.

"Mark Zint was pretty big," Christopher said, with the certainty of someone who must have watched his shows. "But it wasn't just the TV specials or the stage shows. He also came up with the Zint Method."

"The Zint Method?" Paige asked with a frown.

"It's a mentalism technique for forcing the selection of particular objects or numbers," Christopher explained. "He says that it builds on fundamental psychological principles to nudge people towards the choices he wants. It's become one of the most reliable methods. I think he even teaches courses to business leaders these days."

Fundamental psychological principles? As someone with a Ph.D. in criminal psychology, Paige found her interest piqued.

"So how does it work?" she asked.

Christopher shrugged. "I wasn't quite interested enough to pay the hundred and fifty dollars to find out. I'm more of a card tricks on the internet for free kind of guy."

Clearly, though, plenty of people *were* interested in whatever secrets Mark Zint had to impart.

The two of them went to the door, and found themselves met by a genuine, old-fashioned butler, complete with fake British accent. Paige found herself wondering if he was an actor employed for the afternoon, or if Mark Zint really did keep a butler around.

"Yes?" he said.

Christopher showed his badge. "FBI. We need to speak to Mr. Zint."

"I will just see if he's available, sir," the butler said. He turned and walked into the house.

Paige looked across to Christopher. "Should we follow him?"

"You know we can't," Christopher said.

That was frustrating. Because they didn't have a warrant, they had to tell a suspect in their murder case that they were there and wait to see if he would deign to see them. That meant that he had all the time in the world, if he wanted, to try to make an escape.

Paige was left watching the interior of his hallway, which had a grand double staircase leading up, and some, frankly, strange decorations. It was very red, with drapes and carpets all in that color, while a chandelier hung with diamond cut crystals above. A painting hung at eye level of a woman in a diamond necklace. Paige got the feeling that Mr. Zint was trying to set up some kind of trick with subliminal messaging, trying to get his guests to think of the queen of diamonds. If that was the level at which he worked, Paige wasn't impressed.

The butler came hurrying back. Paige half expected him to say that Mark Zint wasn't prepared to speak to them, which would mean they would need to get a warrant to do it. Based on what they had, particularly the death threat, they *might* be able to do it, but it was by no means guaranteed.

"Mr. Zint will see you now," the butler said, to Paige's surprise. "He is entertaining guests, but would be happy for you to join them."

The butler led the way through the house, over parquet flooring that made her shoes click against it. Taxidermy animals decorated many of the walls, while the artwork in between looked expensive, but also featured so many scantily clad women that Paige was sure that was the reason it had been chosen, rather than anything to do with it being painted in the classical period.

They arrived in a large lounge with huge windows on one side so that it was halfway to being a conservatory. Bookcases stood around the walls, although they had at least as many magical props on them as books. A large aquarium stood among the shelves, with turtles swimming back and forth. It seemed that Mark Zint had experience in dealing with sea creatures.

There was classical music playing in the background, while five men were clustered around a table, playing cards with drinks set out in front of them. One of them looked over as they approached, thirty something, dark haired and dark eyed, with a bright smile that didn't quite reach those eyes.

Paige recognized Mark Zint from pictures of him online. They all kept playing for a couple of hands, leaving the two of them standing there waiting. Paige guessed that it was a game designed to assert some kind of authority over her and Christopher, and she had to resist the urge to just interrupt. She suspected that wouldn't get answers. She found herself watching Zint and his expressions, watching the way tension flickered over his face, how his eyebrow raised a fraction later.

Finally, Zint deigned to talk to them.

"Agent Marriott, Agent King, it's good to meet you," he said, slurring the words slightly and then taking a sip of scotch. "I wasn't going to let you in, but then I thought that you might liven things up a little around here." He looked over to Paige, and she had the sensation of being looked over in detail by the magician. "You especially, Agent King."

"I'm glad we could brighten up your day," Paige said. "But we're here to talk about a serious matter, Mr. Zint. Maybe we could talk in private?"

"And leave my guests without me?" Zint said. "Nonsense. Come on, join us. We're playing five card stud."

"We're here on work, Mr. Zint," Christopher said. "It really is important that we speak with you."

Zint shrugged. "Does that mean that you can't have fun while you're doing it? Come on, join me. My butler will get you a drink. You want a drink, don't you, Agent King. You can almost taste it."

Paige noticed him tapping his fingers on the table as he spoke, as if to emphasize certain words.

"No, but I'll play cards if you want," Paige said. It seemed like the best way to get their suspect to talk right then.

"Shall we start with a card trick?" Zint said. "You think of a card, and if I guess it, you have to tell me something about yourself that you haven't told someone else."

"The queen of diamonds?" Paige guessed with a smile. "I spotted your cues on the way in, Mr. Zint. We need to talk to you about Sienna Niven."

"It would be so much more fun to talk about you," Zint said. "Come on, play with us."

Paige sighed and let him deal her in. "If I win, will you talk to us about Sienna?"

"You think you're going to win?"

"Well, you do have a tell," Paige said.

Zint smiled at that. "You think so?"

Paige shrugged. "I don't mean the twitch of your eyebrows. That's obviously deliberate. But you have tension at the corners of your mouth when you have a bad hand that *isn't* deliberate."

"You think you can read me?" For a moment or two, Zint looked angry, then almost amused. "I feel a really strong connection to you, Agent King. I'm sure you should have a drink with me. Or maybe we could see one another later when you're not at work."

Again, he was tapping the table at intervals, as if to emphasize particular words. Paige realized what he was doing.

"Mr. Zint, trying some subliminal hypnosis nonsense isn't going to work," Paige said. "I'm not in the mood for cheap psychological tricks. We're here investigating a murder."

"Cheap psychological tricks?" Zint said. "I've studied human psychology deeper than anyone you've met, Agent."

Paige saw Christopher smile at that. "I feel I should point out that Agent King has a Ph.D. in it, Mr. Zint."

"Then we have so much in common," Zint said.

"Is this how it starts for you with women, Mr. Zint?" Paige asked. "Do you try to use techniques from your act to manipulate them into seeing you? Is that what you tried with Sienna Niven?"

"Do you know the problem with today's culture?" Zint demanded, standing. "A man can't say anything nice about a woman! He can't pay her a compliment, or show her that he's interested in her. And if he dares to while he's in the public eye, he finds himself canceled."

"You still seem to be doing quite well," Paige said.

"That's because people appreciate the advances I've made. I've put together a unique blend of NLP, operant conditioning, suggestion, hypnosis, and choice funneling that works just as well in the boardroom as it does on the stage. *That's* why people pay me a fortune to work with their companies. Do they pay you like that, Miss Ph.D.?"

He'd gone from trying to hit on Paige to being nasty in a matter of moments. It showed just how quickly he might have turned on Sienna.

"What about Mylene Jacques, or Clarissa Bale?" Christopher said, obviously trying to push past Zint's attempts at deflection. "Do those names mean anything to you?"

"I think I saw them on the news," Zint said.

"They were murdered as well, Mark," Paige said. "Have you ever met them? Have you had the kind of conflict with them that you had with Sienna?"

Christopher had his own question at almost the same moment.

"Where were you last night, Mr. Zint? Were you out in any Las Vegas clubs? Did you go to a storage facility to take receipt of a tank full of sharks?"

"What kind of question is that?"

Paige wasn't sure whether he meant her question or Christopher's.

Zint stood up. "This is getting boring. Come on, both of you. You're upsetting my guests. If you're not going to have a drink, then I'm not sure that I want you here anymore."

"Mr. Zint," Christopher said. "If you won't answer any of our questions, you have to realize how suspicious that looks."

"It's not my problem if you can't do your jobs," Zint said.

"Mr. Zint, I'm going to give you one last chance," Christopher said. "We have evidence of you making a death threat towards one of the dead women. You have the skills and the opportunity to have carried out the murders. If you won't provide an alibi here, I'll bring you in and see if you do so in an interrogation room."

"You don't want to do that," Zint said. "My lawyers will destroy you." He looked over to Paige. "Of course, *you'll* be only too happy, won't you? Another woman trying to take down a successful man. That's all this is. Another witch hunt!"

Christopher moved towards Zint, and Paige wasn't sure if the magician threw a punch at him or just staggered drunkenly in Christopher's direction. Either way, Christopher twisted out of the way of the movement, slamming Zint face down onto the card table, sending playing cards scattering. His guests jumped back from the table, but mostly they looked faintly satisfied, as if they'd always kind of hoped that something like this would happen to their host.

“That’s enough,” Christopher said. “I’m done trying to be patient with you. Mark Zint, you’re under arrest.”

CHAPTER TWENTY ONE

Paige looked through the one way glass of the interrogation room at their suspect, trying to read what she could from Mark Zint's body language while she and Christopher waited for him to sober up. Was he worried that they were going to find him out? Were there flashes of guilt as he thought about what he'd done?

Mostly, he just looked angry and frustrated, like he couldn't quite believe that he was there.

Christopher and Detective Sanchez were standing there with Paige, both looking on as if waiting for the perfect moment to go in and speak to Zint.

"So you actually arrested Mark Zint?" Detective Sanchez said. "Please tell me that you have something on him. A rich guy like him will just love making trouble if you don't."

"Plenty of circumstantial things that make him a good suspect," Christopher said. "He made threats towards Sienna Niven after trying to hit on her. He has a past history of sexually harassing women. He's a noted magician, so he has a link to that side of the case. He even keeps fish. Then there's the part where he did his best to avoid answering any questions about the case. He certainly avoided providing an alibi. It was enough to bring him in."

"I guess so," Sanchez said. "I'm the one who will have to live with the repercussions of all of this if you're wrong about him, though. His lawyers are already on the way."

She was obviously thinking that finding herself as the unofficial liaison to the FBI agents on the case wasn't working out quite the way she'd hoped. Paige imagined that she would feel a lot better about it once Paige and Christopher finally cracked the case.

The place to start with that, as far as Paige could see, was by trying to get a confession out of Mark Zint.

"Has he sobered up enough to take a run at, do you think?" Paige asked.

Christopher shrugged. "I don't think he was that drunk to begin with. He's just an asshole when he's sober."

"Ok," Paige said. "Then let me go in there. We might as well try to get something from him before he asks for a lawyer."

"Alone?" Christopher looked a little surprised by that. "Do you think that's a good idea, Paige? It's not as if he showed you much respect back at his place."

This wasn't about respect, though. It was about getting answers.

"Maybe that can play into my hands," Paige said. "It's obvious that he thinks he's superior to me. Maybe I can use that to get him to start talking, if he feels he has to prove something to me. At the very least, he doesn't think I'm a threat."

Christopher didn't look entirely happy about it, almost as if he didn't want her going into a room with a potentially dangerous criminal alone, but he nodded.

"All right," Christopher said. "But we'll both be watching from out here. If he gets out of line, then I'll be straight in there."

Paige was grateful for the concern, but also didn't want it to come to that. She wanted to prove to Christopher that she could handle herself, and deal with this kind of thing without him having to step in to save her.

Paige walked into the interrogation room, taking a seat opposite Mark Zint and starting a recording device.

"Are you ready to talk to us yet, Mark?" Paige asked.

"You think you're clever, dragging me here?" Zint countered. "My lawyers will have me out of here in an instant. They'll make all of this disappear!"

"The way they did with the allegations that Sienna Niven made against you?" Paige asked. "She was one of the women, wasn't she, Mark? You were stalking her. You were obsessed with her."

"Obsessed with an ugly bitch with a big black mark on her face?" Zint said. He laughed, but the laugh came across as fake. She *wanted* me to be obsessed. She wanted to reel me in and tease me so that she could get to my money, but when I asked her to actually put out, she ran away pretty quick."

"So you were trying to have a relationship with her?" Paige asked.

"Aren't you listening?" Zint demanded. "*She* was the one who was trying to have a relationship. That's all women do. They come onto you, tease you, and then try to take advantage. Like you."

Paige raised an eyebrow. "Like me, Mr. Zint?"

"You think I didn't notice you flirting with me back at my place?" Zint said. "The way you were looking at me, the way you were trying to spar with me verbally. What was offering to play cards with me? Something they taught you in FBI training? Get the guys into you, and they'll answer all your questions?"

Paige would have laughed then if it hadn't been so obvious that Zint was serious. Was this what he'd done with all the women who'd accused him of harassing them? Had he simply decided that they were into him? That they were somehow trying to get his attention? Was his own arrogance really that great?

"Let's focus on Sienna," Paige said. "You sent her a message saying that you were planning to kill her."

"I didn't mean it, obviously!" Zint said. "God, why are people so *literal* these days? Besides, she deserved it. She'd told her story to some online news site, making me look like some kind of creep."

Paige had seen this kind of behavior when she'd interviewed psychopaths. Nothing in the world was their fault. The world existed for them, and anything that got in their way was inherently evil, maybe even to be destroyed. There was a level of narcissism to many of them that wouldn't accept that other people might have valid concerns or opinions that differed from theirs, even about their own lives.

"You know," Zint said. "You're pretty easy to read. What was it for you? Broken home? Daddy left? No, more than that. Daddy *died*. Ah, I see now. He died, and you've spent your life since trying to live up to what you think he would have wanted for you. Trying to be the big, tough FBI agent. It hasn't worked, though, has it? You feel doubts sometimes, wonder if you're good enough for all of this. You wonder if you really fit in, or if your colleagues accept you."

Paige sighed, quite deliberately. "I might not know much about magic, but I know about cold reading, and about guessing until something hits home. If you're hoping to impress me, why not try something else? Like giving me an alibi for last night?"

"Why should I have to give you an alibi?" Zint said. "I haven't done anything. I'm sick of people just accusing me of things. Are you planning to go to the press with your little accusations about me? Are you going to try to damage my reputation more?"

Paige was starting to get the impression that Mark Zint really was delusional. She tried to go off in new directions, trying to get any information she could out of him.

"I noticed that you have an aquarium in your home," she said. "Did you get the creatures there from Exotic Aquatics, by any chance?"

Paige wasn't interested in the answer so much as in how Zint reacted when she said the name of the store. He flinched slightly as she said it, as if there were something there that he was worried about. As if he didn't want her asking more.

"What is it, Mark?" she asked. "What is it about the name of that store that makes you react? Maybe it's because you bought a tank full of sharks there yesterday?"

That got a look of surprise, as if he'd been expecting something else. It was an intriguing reaction, and not exactly the one that Paige had been expecting.

"You clearly have some relationship with that store," Paige said. "So what is it?"

"I don't have to answer any of your questions," Zint said. "You don't have any proof of anything. Just guesswork."

"It's true that you don't have to answer," Paige said. "But if you keep refusing to tell us anything, it just makes you look more guilty. Tell me about Clarissa Bale. What about Mylene Jacques?"

With each name, she found herself watching Zint's face, trying to see if there was any reaction. Did he know them? It was impossible to be sure.

"You want me to admit to knowing two dead women now?" he said. "I bet they were just as bad as Sienna. I bet they deserved everything they got."

The more Paige heard from him, the less she liked him, but she still didn't have the proof she needed. She certainly didn't have the confession she might have hoped for.

"I think I'd like my lawyer now," Zint said.

It meant that Paige had to step outside, waiting while Zint made a call to get one in there.

She wasn't entirely surprised when a woman in a sharp suit eventually showed up at the interrogation room. She was in her fifties, with dark hair, steel gray eyes, and sharp features that didn't have a hint of give to them.

It occurred to Paige that he'd probably gotten a woman as a lawyer deliberately, right around the time the sexual harassment allegations started to land. It was a fairly transparent tactic that had become far too common, trying to tell juries and the media that, if one woman trusted him, he couldn't be that bad.

"Allison Savage. I'm Mr. Zint's legal counsel. I want to know on what grounds you're holding my client."

Christopher stepped in then, obviously deciding that if Zint got backup, Paige should have some too.

"On the grounds that he fits the profile of a serial killer we're hunting for, that he sent death threats to one of the victims, and that he refuses to provide an alibi for the time of her murder," Christopher said.

"And do you have any physical evidence to tie him to this murder?" the lawyer asked.

"Once we have his DNA and prints, we'll compare them to anything found at the crime scenes."

"And have you *found* those things at the crime scenes?"

Christopher hesitated just for a moment, obviously not willing to come out with the truth in front of the lawyer. Zint was quick to pick up on it.

"That's a no, Allison. Classic denial body language."

"Then you don't have enough to keep holding my client," the lawyer said.

Paige was worried then. Were they going to have to let Zint go in spite of everything that pointed to him? That didn't seem right. Apparently, Christopher felt the same.

"We get to question your client for twenty-four hours," he said. "I intend to use every minute of that. Or he can give us some answers now and save us all the trouble. Get him to give us an alibi, and he can walk out of here. Otherwise, I have to think that he's hiding something."

The lawyer looked over to Christopher.

"I'll ask, but my client has already made it clear to me on the phone that he would rather not answer questions."

"Why not?" Paige asked. "What is he afraid of?"

The lawyer answered after a moment or two.

"My client has been hounded unfairly by both the press and the police. He has seen his life torn apart by vile, false allegations. Now, you are leveling more allegations at him without any real proof beyond some vague suspicions. If you don't understand why he might not want to cooperate with you, Agent, then you are far too naïve to be doing your job."

Paige looked over to Christopher, and then to the door. He nodded, and the two of them stepped back to let the lawyer talk to her client. The two of them headed to where Detective Sanchez was waiting.

"This isn't looking good," Sanchez said. "The lawyer's right. Without physical evidence, you don't have anything. All he has to do is keep silent, and even if it's suspicious as hell, you can't hold him forever."

"I'll get something out of him," Christopher promised.

Paige hoped so, because otherwise, there was a real risk that a murderer might walk free.

CHAPTER TWENTY TWO

Paige stayed out of the interrogation room this time, watching while Christopher went in to try to make another run at Mark Zint. At the same time, she started to look through everything she could find on him, trying to find something that they might be able to use as leverage to get him to talk.

"Is there a reason that you and Agent Marriott don't want to be in the same room together?" Detective Sanchez asked.

That caught Paige by surprise. She hadn't thought that it was that obvious. Although the detective had it the wrong way around. The problem wasn't that Paige wanted to stay away from Christopher, but that she wanted to be far too close to him.

"We're just taking different approaches to this case," Paige said. She really didn't want to go into the details of what was actually happening between the two of them, or everything she felt.

"Is that all it is?" Detective Sanchez asked. "Usually a partner is there to back their partner up."

"It's... complicated," Paige said. She couldn't help looking over towards Christopher in the interview room as she said it.

"Complicated, sure. It looks pretty simple from where I'm standing. What? You think you're the first person to feel something for her partner?"

Those words sent a thrill of fear through Paige, because if Sanchez could see all that at a glance, how much would Christopher see?

"That's not an option," Paige said. "He's a married man."

"So don't do anything, then," Sanchez said. "But you can't be in this weird in between place where you can't do your job."

"Drop it, Sanchez. We need to focus on getting a conviction."

Sanchez didn't' look comfortable with that. She looked as though she wanted to ask more, but that wasn't going to help the case. It wasn't going to make a difference.

"Just so long as the two of you can actually work together," Sanchez said. "Whatever you think or feel about one another, you're partners. I don't know how it works in the FBI, but here, that means that you have to be there for one another, ready to back one another up, whatever happens. That can't happen if the two of you can barely stand to be in the same room."

Paige knew that the detective had a point, but it wasn't a point she wanted to discuss right then. She wanted to focus on Mark Zint.

She started looking deeper into him, trying to find out more about him. She scoured what she could find of his social media, looking for one comment from Clarissa Bale or Mylene Jacques, one hint that he knew either of the women.

It was obvious that he was self-obsessed, and had a problem with women. He'd sent a death threat to Sienna Niven, but they needed more than that. They needed either proof or a confession, and it seemed pretty clear from what Paige could see through the one way mirror that they weren't even close to a confession.

"Let's talk about your day yesterday," Christopher said. "How did that go?"

"Fine," Zint replied.

"Walk me through that day."

"My client has already said that he has no wish to provide an alibi," his lawyer put in.

"I'm more interested in whether he went to a storage facility used by online sellers," Christopher said.

"Why would I go anywhere like that when I have a mansion where I can receive things?" Zint countered. "Do you have a mansion, Agent Marriott? What do they pay you in the FBI for asking stupid questions?"

He was being deliberately combative, obviously enjoying this. He probably thought that there was no way that the FBI were ever going to find enough to charge him. Paige couldn't make up her mind if that was a sign of a man who was guilty, taunting them, or a man who wasn't but was simply so narcissistic that he wanted to make this whole thing about him.

The trouble was, he might be right about them not finding enough to charge him. Paige couldn't find any comments by Mylene or Clarissa on any of Zint's social media posts, and a quick search through their social media didn't show any posts about him or messages to him either.

That worried Paige a little. If it were just Sienna who had been killed, then maybe that obvious connection would be enough, but with three victims, Paige needed evidence of a connection to all three.

With Zint, it would be messages, wouldn't it? He'd stalked Sienna at least partly online, and he hadn't been shy about sending her messages, even threats. Yet there wasn't anything like that for the other two victims. Paige would have picked it up in her first pass through their social media if there were.

Had he met them in real life? Had he hit on them in clubs he went to, or at his shows? There was no evidence that either of the women had been to his shows, and Paige expected most people to announce that kind of thing on their social media, but maybe these two were outliers.

"I want to talk about Clarissa Bale and Mylene Jacques," Christopher said.

"Well, I don't," Zint replied.

Christopher pressed on regardless. "Did you know them? Did you ever have any contact, in person or online, with either Clarissa Bale or Mylene Jacques?"

Paige watched Zint's face again as Christopher talked about them. She realized something as she watched. He wasn't showing quite the same anger at their names as he showed when Christopher and Paige had mentioned Sienna before. Oh, there was the performance of it, the snarling and the pretense that he was above all this. There was some general animosity, but no more than he'd displayed towards Paige. He might not have reacted with surprise at their names, but he hadn't displayed the kind of hatred that he obviously had for Sienna, even now that she was dead.

Paige went looking online, trying to work out who the women had been who had leveled allegations of sexual harassment against him. That search quickly ran into a dead end. Some of the names were out there, published on message boards along with their details, doxing them so that they could be targeted by those who were prepared to take their support for Mark Zint to extremes. Others had managed to remain anonymous, or had perhaps been required to after they'd settled their allegations out of court.

Either way, it was possible that the two dead women were among those who had made allegations. It was impossible to know for sure either way.

"Ok, you don't want to talk about the women?" Christopher said. "Then let's talk about magic tricks."

"Are you going to ask me for all my secrets?" Zint said. "I saw the way you looked around my house like a fanboy. That's what you are, isn't it, Agent Marriott? How many times have you watched my shows? No, don't tell me, I'm sure it's plenty."

He didn't give Christopher a chance to give a real answer. Paige guessed that was a deliberate power move, designed to take control of the conversation. He was playing games with them, and enjoying this far too much.

Paige called up the security footage from the storage facility. It could have been him there, she had to admit, but there was nothing definitive that meant that they would be able to prove it to a jury. It could just as easily have been another man.

The more that Paige looked at Mark Zint answering questions, the more doubts she found herself having that it actually was him who had done this. He was an obnoxious man, and clearly one who treated women poorly whenever he thought that he could get away with it, but Paige couldn't find anything that definitively linked him to the murders. Yes, he was a former magician, but in Las Vegas, that wasn't unique. Yes, he owned an aquarium full of unusual sea life, but if Exotic Aquatics was anything to go by, plenty of people were willing to pay for that kind of thing.

Then there was that lack of reaction. That bothered Paige more than all the rest of it.

"Actually," Christopher said. "I wanted to ask you if you'd spent any time exploring classic stage magic. Have you ever done a version of the bullet catch trick, for example?"

"Russian roulette where an audience member knows which chamber is loaded is more impressive," Zint said. "But yes, I've dabbled in the classics."

"What about escapology?"

"Where are you going with this?" his lawyer demanded.

"I'm just trying to see if Mr. Zint has any familiarity with the tricks copied in the course of the murders," Christopher replied.

Zint rounded on him. "They're some of the most classic effects in magic. Every magician in this town knows how they work. I guess even a hobbyist like you does. Knowing about them doesn't prove anything."

Paige could hear the frustration there. Apparently, so could Christopher.

"Mr. Zint, you can leave at any time. All you have to do is provide us with an alibi for last night. Tell us where you were. Tell us if you went anywhere near any storage facilities, or near a community art collective's theater."

"You think I'm going to trust you?" Zint said. "I know how this works. Everything I say and do gets twisted against me."

"I'll give you some time to consider," Christopher said, and came through into the space beyond the interrogation room. He looked frustrated. "This will take time. A man like that, it's going to take a while. I need anything you can give me to help get him to crack."

Paige shook her head. "There isn't anything that I've been able to find. There's nothing that definitively proves he had any contact with Mylene Jacques or Clarissa Bale."

"He's obviously hiding something, though."

"He is," Paige agreed. "But I'm not sure that it's about him being the murderer."

Christopher frowned at her. So did Detective Sanchez.

"What do you mean?" Christopher asked. "Did you find something that shows he isn't?"

Paige shook her head. "Nothing like that. But I've been watching him. He doesn't react the same way to Mylene or Clarissa's names that he does to Sienna's. There's no evidence that he has a real connection to them. Yes, he's a jerk, but I'm not sure that's enough to make him a murderer."

"Before we went to his house, you were as convinced as I was," Christopher said. "More."

"I know," Paige replied. "But his reactions-"

"He could be *faking* those reactions," Christopher said. "Like he did when he tried to play cards with you."

"And I saw through that," Paige pointed out.

Christopher obviously wasn't buying it, though. "He's our best suspect, Paige. Everything about him screams that he's the killer. Look, if you don't have anything on him, that's fine, but don't tell me it isn't him. I'm going back in there to take another run at him."

"Christopher…" Paige began, but he was already heading back into the interrogation room.

It seemed that he'd made up his mind. Paige wished that she was as convinced, but right then, she simply wasn't. And, if Zint wasn't the killer, then that meant that the real killer might still be out there somewhere, already plotting his next murder.

Paige needed to find something that would point them towards him. Something that would, at least, convince Christopher that they were looking in the wrong place.

Something that Mark Zint had said caught Paige's attention then. He'd talked about Sienna being ugly because of a black mark on her face, but there hadn't been any trace of that mark when she'd been found, had there? It was incongruous, and even if it might prove to be nothing, Paige felt as though that kind of incongruity was her best chance of getting all of this back on track.

She stood, grabbing her laptop.

"Where are you going?" Detective Sanchez asked. "We're still in the middle of an interrogation."

"You and Christopher have things here," Paige said. "If he asks where I've gone, tell him that I'm heading to the morgue."

CHAPTER TWENTY THREE

Paige stood outside the Las Vegas City morgue, taking deep breaths until she could work up the courage to enter. She knew that this next part was going to be hard, and it took several seconds to steel herself for it.

Paige had seen bodies at crime scenes before. She had even seen Sienna Niven's body, but that didn't make it easier to walk in there, with the prospect of having to look over three corpses ahead of her. Looking down at her father's dead form had been the moment that changed Paige's life and sent her down the path of looking into the world of serial killers. The prospect of having to do it again now with the three victims in this case filled her with a kind of dread.

"Did you lose someone?"

Paige turned to see a young man approaching, heading for the doors. He had a name badge already pinned to his shirt, suggesting that he worked there.

She wasn't sure how to answer. She *had* lost someone, but her father's death wasn't relevant to this. All that mattered right now was trying to find answers in the case. Paige's feelings of dread didn't enter into it.

Except that it was still hard, even knowing that.

Paige took out her badge. "I'm Agent King, with the FBI. I'm here in connection with the murders of Sienna Niven, Mylene Jacques, and Clarissa Bale."

"Ah, right, sorry," the young man said. "I'm Michael, one of the coroner's staff here at the morgue. You just had that look that people get when they have to come here to identify someone they love."

Paige didn't want to go into everything in her past that had given her that look. She didn't want this guy who worked in the morgue to think about her as just another family member of a victim. She wanted him to be clear that she was a highly trained agent, there to do a job.

"I need to see the bodies of the victims," Paige said.

"You'd better come inside, Agent," the young man said, and led the way into the morgue.

Inside, the waiting area seemed to be almost like that of a hospital or a dentist, with the same medical feel offset by pastel colors, cheap prints on the walls and magazines left waiting on small tables. It was all much colder than the heat outside, and there was a faint scent that Paige knew was probably formaldehyde.

"If you wait here for a moment," the young man said, gesturing to some comfortable looking chairs. "I'll get the coroner to come talk to you."

Paige sat there, waiting and doing her best to ignore the leaflets set out there offering support, or providing the details of therapists who were no doubt waiting to take the money of grieving families. Paige had spent more than her share of time in therapy after her father's death. That had been the other part of what had pushed her towards psychology. She'd started out wanting to understand herself, and then had found that she wanted to understand serial killers far more.

She was starting to feel that she might understand this one, but she wanted to be sure. It had all come down to the comment Mark Zint had made about Sienna having a black mark on her face. If Paige remembered correctly, Clarissa Bale had a beauty mark. Mylene Jacques didn't have an obvious one, but she *had* been wearing a lot of makeup. That makeup might easily conceal such a thing.

Paige wasn't sure what it meant, but she was sure that it meant *something*. First, though, she had to make sure that she was right about her hunch. Doing that meant seeing the body for herself.

An older man came into the waiting area through the door where the younger man had gone to fetch him. He was wearing a slightly old-fashioned suit and looked as if he were getting ready to go to out somewhere rather than work on the dead. He was probably sixty or so, maybe older, with white hair and hands that seemed gnarled until Paige wondered how he was able to hold his medical instruments.

"You're Agent King?" he asked, sounding slightly surprised by it, as if he still hadn't caught onto the possibility that women could be FBI agents.

"I am," Paige said, showing her badge. "I'm one of the agents looking into the murders of Clarissa Bale, Mylene Jacques, and Sienna Niven."

"I'm Dr. Benjamin, the coroner here. And you're here because…"

"Because I need to look at them," Paige said. "There's something I need to check that might be relevant to the investigation."

"I'm sorry, Agent King, but as I told Michael, I'm just about to leave for the day."

That took Paige a little aback.

"Sir, I'm working to catch a killer here."

"And you want me to believe that, if you get to see the deceased, then you'll find something that will suddenly allow you to do that?"

Paige nodded. She hoped that if she found a way to explain it, then Dr. Benjamin would help.

"I think I've found something about one of the victims that, if it's true for the others, will help to establish the pattern of the serial killer doing this. That might be enough to let me work out who he might target next, or even find out who he is."

The coroner didn't look entirely impressed. "In general, Agent, the way this works is that *I'm* the one who looks at the bodies of the deceased. You have my preliminary reports on the first two victims, and you'll have my report on Sienna Niven soon enough."

Paige hadn't been expecting any resistance here. She'd been expecting this part to go smoothly, so that she would have her answers quickly.

"Sir, I'm trying to establish something important here," Paige said.

"And what is that?" Dr. Benjamin asked. "What exactly is it that you think you'll find?"

"A suspect mentioned that Sienna Niven had a black mark on her face. If I recall from the crime scene photographs, Clarissa Bale also had a beauty mark. If that's true for all three women…"

"*That's* what you want to drag me back in there to check? Some conjecture that at best points to a vague physical similarity between the three victims?" Dr. Benjamin didn't look happy. "No, Agent King. I simply don't have the time right now."

"I'm in the middle of a murder investigation," Paige pointed out.

"Agent King, do you know what it's like, working as the coroner here?" Dr. Benjamin asked.

Paige got the feeling that he was going to tell her.

"I get bodies coming in at all hours of the day and night. My team and I work hard on them, trying to get answers, using all the expertise that I've built up through a medical degree and years of experience."

That seemed to be his way of reminding Paige that he'd been doing his job much longer than she'd been doing hers.

"And all the time, I have police, and now federal agents, making calls, or showing up, insisting that their case is more important than all the others, that they need special attention. If I gave in to all of that, I would be here until midnight every night."

"This will take five minutes, and it potentially allows us to catch a serial killer," Paige pointed out. She couldn't believe that the coroner wasn't prepared to do even that much for her.

"Potentially, possibly, probably," Dr. Benjamin said. "That all sounds like you're just guessing, young lady. Now, I'm on my way to dinner with a state representative, in which I'll be trying to argue for more funding for the coroner's department. *That* is a much better use of my time than indulging some hunch of yours."

He turned from Paige and walked from the morgue, leaving Paige to stare at his back in frustration. She couldn't believe that the coroner would be so unhelpful when there was an active murder investigation, whatever his supposed justifications.

Paige was still standing there when the young man who had shown her in, Michael, came out. He was wearing scrubs now, and nodded to Paige.

"Did you get what you needed?" he asked.

"No," Paige said in frustration. "Your coroner decided that it was more important to go to dinner than to help me out with the case."

"Ah," Michael said. "Dr. Benjamin can be like that sometimes. If you come back in the morning-"

"Someone else might be dead by then," Paige said. "This killer has killed twice in two days now. If he's on a spree, there's every chance that he might kill again tonight."

She could see how uncomfortable Michael looked at that. It was nothing compared to the frustration Paige felt, and the helplessness of potentially not being able to catch a serial killer.

"Look," Michael said. "What is it exactly that you need? I'm not really in a position to conduct a full examination without the coroner present."

"Just to see the bodies, specifically their faces," Paige said, feeling a hint of hope.

"I… might be able to help with that," Michael said. He gestured to the doors he'd come through. "Come on. This way."

He led the way through into a large examination room. There were rows of storage for the dead around the walls, behind numbered doors.

"You want Sienna Niven, Clarissa Bale, and Mylene Jacques, right?" he said.

Paige nodded. "That's right."

He went around to the shelves, opening the doors in turn. The cold was palpable now, and Paige wanted to believe that was the reason why she was suddenly shivering. She forced herself to look down at Sienna Niven's face as Michael uncovered it.

In that moment, she could have been back in the forest again, looking down at her father. Paige had to remind herself that she was there to do a job, that she had a killer to catch.

That brought things back into focus enough for her to stare at the lines of Sienna's features, taking in the large dark mole just below her cheekbone, like an accent offsetting the beauty of the rest.

She walked over to Clarissa Bale next. Sure enough, she had a beauty mark too, this one smaller, but definitely visible. Paige took a breath and headed over to Mylene Jacques.

She still had her makeup in place, which was a little surprising. Hadn't the coroner bothered to remove it during his examination?

"Can you remove her makeup?" Paige asked Michael.

"I don't know if-"

"Please, I need to see if she has a beauty mark like the others."

The coroner's assistant hesitated for a second or two, but then nodded, returning with a set of wipes that he used to delicately remove the makeup from Mylene Jacques's features.

There, on her left cheek, Paige saw a beauty mark. Just like the others.

CHAPTER TWENTY FOUR

He met Antoinette at the entrance to the old park, the place where his father had debuted so many of his tricks, out on the large stage that stood in the middle, and where he'd been so abusive and cruel about everything. Where Antoinette had been, too. That was why she was here now:

To pay for it.

"Wow," Antoinette said. "When you said you wanted to meet here, I wasn't sure what to expect. This is… so run down."

It was. Once, the park had been bright and vibrant, well cared for, even an attraction. Once, families had come there to sit on the grass, walk between the trees, and watch the shows put on there.

Now, the park was an overgrown skeleton of what it had once been. The foliage had grown out of control, while chains hung across the paths at intervals to try to keep people out. The whole place had changed beyond recognition.

Antoinette looked the same, though. Well, more or less. Older, certainly, but still as slender, still with bottle blonde hair and a tan that had been worked on in a salon. Still with those cold blue eyes that had always looked through him before like he was nothing. She'd obviously had work done, a facelift, perhaps, maybe a little Botox, but the beauty mark on her chin was still there, as if she saw it like some badge of honor.

"It's good to see you again, Stephen," she said, throwing her arms around him as if there had always been affection between them. As if she hadn't seduced his father and gotten between them so that any hint of love he had for his son disappeared. She held him out at arm's length. "It's still amazing to believe the man you've become. I remember when you were just a boy. You look just like your father."

Those words were almost enough to make him lash out at her blindly, but he forced himself to hold back. He had already decided how Antoinette was going to die, after all.

"While you look exactly the same," Stephen said. It wasn't a compliment, but Antoinette appeared to take it as one. She'd always been vain.

"You're very kind," she said. "But why invite me here, of all places? We could have met up for dinner somewhere nice. I know you have the money for it these days."

No thanks to her. She'd been the one left everything when his father died. Stephen had been the one who'd had to rebuild his life. He'd found success, too, until things had fallen apart. His marriage, his company, all of it gone.

He'd run back to Las Vegas to find out if it held any answers for him. It turned out that it had. He'd stood in the middle of his father's workshop and known what he had to do. He'd had the space and the money for it. He'd just needed to *act*.

"We can go to dinner another time," he lied. "For now… well, I found some things that brought back memories. I thought you might want to see them."

"Here?" Antoinette said.

"Just trust me."

"Ok," Antoinette said, although she didn't sound as enthusiastic about it as she had about the prospect of dinner.

Stephen moved towards the park, leading the way under the chains.

"It's just this way," Stephen said. The interior of the park was kind of a maze, the chains and the overgrown plants cutting off some paths, forming others.

The whole place was lit now by candles Stephen had put in place in lanterns, each one throwing strange shadows over the surrounding parkland.

"Do you remember the shows we put on here?" Antoinette asked. "I remember once we did the sword box, and your father almost stabbed you."

"He *did* stab me," Stephen corrected her. It had been meant to be Antoinette in the box, but she'd complained of a pulled muscle before the show, so he'd been the one who'd had to go in, regardless of the fact that he hadn't memorized the positioning required to stay safe quite so thoroughly.

"Oh, it was just a graze," Antoinette said. "Don't be so dramatic."

He'd needed seventeen stitches, but Stephen guessed that Antoinette wasn't interested in that. She tended not to be interested in anything other than herself.

"Talking of dramatic…" Stephen said instead as the two of them entered the heart of the park.

This was the spot where the stage stood, dilapidated as the rest of the place, but Stephen had done his best with it. Stephen had dressed that stage carefully. He'd picked out tricks that had hurt him over the years deliberately, from the vanishing doors to the dekolta chair, the rope trick to the knife through the hand. Every one of them was a reminder of the lengths his father had gone to for fame.

The box and the saw sat at the heart of it all, carefully lit by spotlights Stephen had put in place for just that effect.

"What is all of this, Stephen?" Antoinette asked, as if she didn't know.

"Can't you guess?" Stephen countered, trying to keep his voice genial.

"These look like a bunch of your father's old props. Why these ones, though?"

Stephen had to work to keep his anger in check. "Don't pretend you don't know."

"Know what?"

"These were ones my father forced me to take part in because *you* always found a way to get out of it. You were sleeping with him, and that meant that you didn't have to do anything that was untested, or dangerous. I always had to instead."

Antoinette gave him a stern look. "Don't be a child, Stephen."

"I *was* a child!" he snarled back at her. "You wrapped him around your little finger, got him to do everything you wanted, and I was the one left doing the work. Well, not after tonight."

Antoinette looked angry now. "You think that's how things were? Because what *I* remember is a bratty teenager, who had a chance to be a part of something big, and spent all his time complaining."

"I was never given a choice about *any* of it," Stephen replied.

Antoinette huffed. "I'm done with this. I thought it would be good to meet up again, but I was wrong. I'm leaving, Stephen."

"No," Stephen said as he advanced on her. "No, you aren't."

CHAPTER TWENTY FIVE

It was getting dark as Paige went back out to the car, determined to find out about any magician with a link to beauty spots. She sat in it with her computer, trying to find answers that she could bring back to Christopher.

Presumably, he was still in the interrogation room, trying to get answers out of Mark Zint. Certainly, he hadn't called her so far, or messaged her to find out what she was doing. Was that because he was so caught up in the interrogation that he hadn't had a chance? Did he simply trust Paige to deal with it? Or did he not care enough to communicate?

That last possibility hurt, even though Paige knew that she had no right for it to hurt. Christopher wasn't obliged to be there with her. He certainly wasn't obliged to care. He was just trying to do his job, and Paige had to do hers.

Once she had enough, she could take it to him, and then they would bring down the serial killer, together.

First, though, Paige had to prove the connection. To do that, Paige had to find a magician with an assistant who had a beauty mark like the ones on Clarissa, Mylene, and Sienna's faces.

The trouble was that searching for that on the internet didn't bring up any immediate results. If there had been such an act, they hadn't been big enough for the information to make a big splash, or they'd failed so thoroughly that it had all ended up buried under the rest of the internet. It meant that Paige found herself having to skim past site after site dedicated to skincare or surgical mole removal.

If there was an answer here, then it was buried pretty deep. Paige knew she had to keep searching, keep trying until she found something, but how long would that take? There had to be a faster way.

Paige tried started trying other searches, looking into the history of magic, specifically around Las Vegas. That brought up a lot of general articles, talking about famous magicians of the past, but it also brought up something more interesting, something that had Paige clicking on it instantly.

The Museum of Las Vegas Magic, dedicated to the history of stage magicians in the city, was only a few blocks off the strip. Paige checked the opening hours. She would have to hurry, but she might still be able to make it.

Throwing the car into gear, she started to speed through the Las Vegas traffic, weaving in and out. They'd trained Paige in the basics of pursuit driving at the FBI academy, but this was Paige's first time putting them into practice, hitting the lights and siren of the car the field office had supplied so that she could move faster through the streets without crashing into anyone.

She had to get to that museum before it closed. This might be her last chance to identify the killer before he was able to strike again.

There was an art to this kind of high-speed driving. It was about thinking ahead, trying to predict what people would do. Most of those there on the street got out of Paige's way, but not all, and that meant that she had to swerve around them, gripping onto the wheel tightly as the car lurched from side to side with the effort of dodging around the traffic.

Paige did everything she could to keep it on course, but it was a struggle. She skidded around a limousine taking people to some kind of party, then darted in between a bus and a truck. Paige made up time along the strip, driving as fast as she dared with people around. This might not be a chase, but it was still life or death if she couldn't get to the museum before all the staff left for the day.

Paige saw it ahead and pulled up in front of it, not caring that she had to more or less abandon the car in the street to do it. The windows were filled with magic paraphernalia, including a display of top hats and masks from down the ages, while posters were stuck everywhere advertising shows around the city.

Steel shutters were rolling down over the doors, and Paige hammered on them, hoping that someone would hear her.

"We're closed!" a voice called from inside.

Paige pressed her badge up against the glass of the door. "FBI! Open up! I need your help!"

For a moment or two, the shutters kept descending, and Paige had to jerk her hand back to avoid being caught by them. Then, though, the shutters reversed direction, a man coming to the door and opening it.

He was perhaps fifty, bald, but with a graying triangle of beard, and multiple earrings in one ear. He wore a tuxedo, presumably in imitation of great magicians of the past, and he was currently looking at Paige as if he expected this whole thing to be some grand hoax at his expense.

"What's all this about?" he demanded.

"I'm Agent Paige King, with the FBI," Paige said, showing her badge again. "Who are you, sir?"

"I'm Herman Weber. I run the museum here."

"Have you heard about the murders in the last couple of days, Mr. Weber? The ones that have copied magical routines?"

"Of course I have," Herman replied. "Everyone in the business has been talking about it."

"I'm working the case, and I need information," Paige said. "Information about magic acts in the city. Is that something you might be able to help with?"

"Well, yes, I suppose so," Herman said. "You'd better come inside."

The interior of the place was filled with glass boxes, each holding what appeared to be props from magic tricks. It looked a little like the workshop where Zane Caister had worked in that respect, only with considerably more order to it.

Herman gestured to a couple of armchairs in one corner. They appeared to be exhibits, but he didn't seem to have any problem sitting in one of them, with Paige opposite him.

"Did you know that these chairs were once used by the amazing Malfini Sisters for their transmogrification effect? For years, people searched for some secret to it hidden in the chairs, but I'm relatively confident at this point that they are just comfortable chairs."

"And you don't mind sitting on your exhibits?" Paige said.

"I like to think it's what Angelique and Katrina would have wanted." He said it as if he'd known them personally. Perhaps he had. Paige really didn't have much of an idea of who any of these people were, even if the museum owner made it sound as if everyone should have heard of them.

"Now," he said. "What can I do for you? If you're looking for information about murderers, I'm afraid that while the magical community can be close knit, it isn't likely that anyone has just come out and admitted something like that."

Paige got the impression that he was a man who liked to talk. A lot.

"I'm looking for a specific magic act," Paige said. "One I don't have a name for. Do you think you might be able to identify them?"

"Perhaps," Herman said. "It will depend on what you can tell me about them. Some acts have signature effects, for example, or particular quirks to their act."

"This one would have featured an assistant with a beauty mark on her face."

She saw Herman frown. "That… isn't much to go on. A beauty mark? Is that all?"

Paige nodded, feeling her hope ebb away. She'd been so excited when she found the connection between the women. It had seemed like the thing that was finally going to lead her to the murderer, but if it wasn't enough to identify a potential killer, then she'd just wasted time she didn't have.

"Hmm…" Herman said. "It *does* ring a faint bell though."

The embers of Paige's hope flickered back into life.

"Can you remember what?" she asked. She needed answers, and she needed them fast.

"It was something in the archives, I think. Follow me."

Herman stood and headed deeper into the museum, with Paige following in his wake, hoping that it would lead to something that she could use. He led the way past exhibits that included an overlarge milk churn and a bed of nails, to a spot where several file cabinets stood in a row against a wall. Herman opened one of them, rooting through it.

"It was… let's see, a few years ago now. There was an act. The Amazing Stupendo, or the Stupendous Amazo, or some such. No, that wasn't it, was it? I remember though that there was an assistant who always dressed like some eighteenth-century court lady, to highlight her beauty spot."

He kept working his way through the cabinet, until finally he pulled out a poster for a show with the same flourish he might have used to pull a rabbit from a hat. He unfolded it carefully.

"The Great Supremus!" Herman said. "That was it. Real name Henry Booth, I believe. He didn't think it had the same ring, although I've always admired magicians with the courage to perform under their own names."

"What happened to him?" Paige asked.

"Oh, he was never terribly successful. Didn't really do anything original, and his whole act was quite cliché. He died a few years ago. From what I understand, his son went off to become some kind of businessman. While his assistant… Antoinette Couchon, that was her name, she hung around on the fringes of the business a little while longer."

"Thank you," Paige said, barely able to contain her excitement. She all but ran for the door. "You might just have helped to save someone's life!"

Paige ran out to the car, where she looked up the names she'd just gotten on her laptop. Sure enough Henry Booth had been a magician, and Antoinette Couchon had been his assistant. He'd died almost ten years ago, when his son Stephen had been fourteen.

Fourteen. The same age Paige had been when she lost her father. She knew how much the pain of losing a father at that age could cause, how much of an impact it could have on a life.

She looked up Stephen. He had a record, for assaulting another kid in a foster home. Yet after he'd gotten out, it appeared that he'd gone straight, starting a business that had rapidly become successful.

Paige quickly found records for it, along with the ones that said he'd divorced a year ago. The DMV's records suggested that he'd moved back to Las Vegas then.

Was he the one killing people now? Had the sudden return to the city brought back whatever hurtful memories he had? Had it pushed him over the edge?

If so, it seemed that he was fixating on women who looked like Antoinette. She had to be in danger, if he hadn't gotten to her already. Somehow, this was all about her, and Paige needed to get to her, to make sure that she was safe, before Stephen managed to kill her.

CHAPTER TWENTY SIX

Paige looked up Antoinette's address with the DMV, then drove to her house as quickly as she dared, not wanting to waste a minute when there was a chance that she was being targeted by a killer.

While she did it, Paige considered whether to call Christopher for backup. After all, she could be heading into a potentially dangerous situation, and standard procedure said not to do that without the assistance of her partner.

Paige didn't call, though, not yet. In spite of the worry that she felt for Antoinette Couchon, she didn't have any real proof that the woman was in immediate danger. Besides, Christopher had already made it clear that he thought Mark Zint was the killer. Paige would need more than a few suspicions based on a facial mark to change his mind.

Besides, she didn't want to have to rely on Christopher for everything. She couldn't just assume that he would be there whenever she wanted. Paige had to deal with some things on her own. She wanted to show *him* that she could deal with them, too.

No, she would go to Antoinette's house, find out more, and *then* call Christopher, if she needed to. This might all be nothing. She might get there and find Antoinette alive and well. She might get there and Antoinette might give her more proof about Stephen, but it might take an hour. Paige couldn't imagine Christopher being patient through that when he had every reason to believe that he already had the killer in custody. He would see that as a waste of time he needed to crack Mark Zint.

No, it was better if Paige did this alone for now. She would find more evidence of what was going on, and only then contact Christopher.

Antoinette's house turned out to be a large house in the suburbs of Las Vegas, looking pretty old by the standards of the city. It was big and well cared for, with roses in the front garden, and a climbing honeysuckle winding its way up a trellis on the front wall. It seemed quite a large place for someone living alone, as if she'd inherited it from someone else, or bought it in expectation of having a large family that never materialized. It stood amid a row of family homes, all with the seemingly obligatory minivan or SUV on the driveway.

Antoinette's driveway was empty, and that simple fact made Paige worry a little. Still, she told herself that it didn't necessarily mean anything. Maybe Antoinette's car was in the shop, or maybe she had gone out for an hour or two with friends.

Paige slid her car into Antoinette's driveway, and found herself readying her gun without thinking about it. She'd only been an agent for a few days now, but she found herself reacting the way she'd been trained, ready for danger.

Paige got out of the car and approached the door, ringing the bell. She stood there waiting, but also listening for any sound that might mean trouble inside, anything that might mean there was already a killer in there.

Paige couldn't hear anything, the silence stretching the seconds around Paige until each one seemed like an eternity.

"Antoinette?" Paige called out, hoping for any kind of response. There was still nothing.

Paige moved around the house now, looking through the windows, checking for any sign that Antoinette might be inside. Even more importantly, she was checking for any sign that the former magician's assistant might be in danger in there.

If it came to that, what would she do? Would she be able to kick in the door, burst in there, and take down the serial killer all alone?

Paige would do anything she had to do to keep this woman safe.

The first thing she needed to do was establish exactly where Antoinette was. Paige took out her phone. She had one advantage in this situation: she wasn't a consultant anymore; she was an agent.

That meant that she had the power to ask for help without going through Christopher. Paige made a call to Quantico, rehearsing what she would say once she got an answer.

"FBI," a voice on the other end of the line said.

"This is Agent Paige King. I'm calling for technical assistance with trying to trace someone. I need a phone number for a woman named Antoinette Couchon, of Las Vegas."

"Give us a moment," the voice on the other end of the line said. "Yes, we have her. Sending the number to your phone now."

Paige's phone pinged with the number. "Um… thank you."

She wasn't used to things happening so fast for her. She was used to having to work for every scrap of information on a case, every hint of insight.

She called Antoinette's number, hoping that she would simply answer, and that Paige would have a slightly embarrassing conversation with a woman who was out seeing a show or dating some guy somewhere in Vegas.

She picked up, briefly, but there wasn't a voice on the other end of the line. No one answered. There was a protected silence instead, as if someone didn't dare to speak, or as if they were simply listening.

"Antoinette? This is Agent King of the FBI."

The line went suddenly, abruptly, dead, cut off so sharply that Paige was almost certain that it was in response to her announcing who she was.

Was that just because Antoinette hadn't wanted to talk to the FBI, or was it because someone else had been there, listening in? Had the killer been there?

In that moment, Paige was terrified for Antoinette's safety. Scared enough that she found herself going around to the rear door of the house, checking it. When it wouldn't open, Paige braced herself, and then kicked the door as hard as she could.

She wasn't a large woman, but Paige still had her full weight behind the kick, and it was enough that she heard the crack of the lock giving way. She had her gun out in an instant as she burst into the house, hoping that Antoinette was safe.

She found herself in a large kitchen, which looked as though it was barely used. It was too pristine, too sterile, as if Antoinette ate out or got takeout most nights.

"Antoinette? Are you in here?" Paige called out. There was no answer, but Paige couldn't leave it at that. She knew that she had to sweep the house. She started to move forward, heading into a living room with furniture that looked a little fussy and old-fashioned, as if it hadn't been updated in a while.

Paige was more concerned with making sure that there wasn't a killer in the house. She made her way through it, heading slowly upstairs with her gun held up ahead of her. She swept each room in turn, pausing at the door to each of the bedrooms, opening each one in turn, and then bursting in, moving quickly to make sure that the room was empty.

Finally, there was only one bedroom left. Paige could feel the tension rising in her. If the killer was anywhere in the house with Antoinette, he was here. She tried the handle, slid the door open, and then burst inside with her weapon raised, ready to fire.

The bedroom was empty.

Paige dared to breathe a sigh of relief, but even as she did so, she felt a twinge of disappointment. She'd been hoping that she could end things here. Now, she still needed to find Antoinette.

Paige called Quantico again.

"This is Agent Paige King. I need an urgent trace on a cell phone number. I believe the phone may belong to someone who is about to be the victim of a killer."

"Give us the number, Agent, and we'll get right on it."

Paige read the number from her own phone, and then waited. It felt like hours before she got a reply, but in fact it must only have been seconds.

"We've narrowed it down to one city block," the tech on the other end of the line said.

In Las Vegas, that was still potentially a lot of places.

"Can you pull up records on those buildings?" Paige asked. "Do any of them look like theatres or performance spaces?"

Those had been the venues where the killer had undertaken his grisly work before, murdering women out on stage as if for an invisible audience. No, Paige realized, she and the others arriving at the scene had been the audience.

And this crime was meant to be the climax. For that, Stephen Booth would choose somewhere special. Somewhere meaningful to him.

"There's one space," the tech said. "An old park. It's disused now, but it seems that there were regular performances there."

Paige froze at the thought of it. "That's the place. I need an address, right away."

"Sending it through to your phone now, Agent."

Just like that, Paige knew where the killer was. He was planning to finish this in a way that made for a big reveal and then… well, then he would probably try to disappear, vanishing into mid-air like one of his tricks.

Paige couldn't allow that, and she *definitely* couldn't allow another woman to be killed. She had to get there before Stephen had a chance to kill Antoinette.

She ran downstairs, moving quickly now as she raced out of the house. Paige sprinted back to her car, threw herself into the driver's seat and punched the address the techs had gotten for her into her GPS.

She set off with a screech of tires, siren blazing to keep traffic out of her way as she drove. Before, she'd been racing to get to the house, but now, Paige was driving at a speed that terrified even herself. She had to make it to the old park before Stephen killed Antoinette. Paige was the only hope the former assistant had of coming through this alive.

Paige called Christopher as she sped along, weaving in and out of traffic, hoping that this time, she might get an answer. It went through to voicemail, though. He was obviously still in his interrogation of Mark Zint. Paige could only hope that he would be done soon, or she was going to have to take on a serial killer alone.

Paige tried to tell herself that she'd done it before. She'd gone to face Adam Riker alone when he'd captured her mother, and she hadn't even been a trained agent then. Even so, Paige found herself wishing that Christopher were there. Paige was the one who found the killers, but Christopher was the one with the skills to take them down.

Faced with Christopher's voicemail Paige did her best to summarize the situation as she drove.

"Christopher, I'm leaving the house of a woman named Antoinette Couchon. She was the assistant to a magician, and she has a facial mark the same as the other victims. I believe that the magician's son, Stephen Booth, may be the killer. I'm currently heading to a performance space in an old park. I'll send you the address. Call me when you get this."

Paige tried to keep the panic she was starting to feel out of her voice, while still conveying a sense of urgency. She had to do this, and if Christopher wasn't there to help, then Paige would just have to do it alone.

She was going to go to the address where Antoinette was. She was going to do everything she could to save her. She was going to take down Stephen Booth. Paige didn't need Christopher's help to do that, because she had more than enough training to do it by herself.

She just really, *really* wished that he were there.

CHAPTER TWENTY SEVEN

Paige pulled up outside the park, drumming her fingers on the steering wheel, trying to work out whether she should head inside. The park seemed to squat in front of her, dark compared to the bright lights of Las Vegas around it. Yet not as dark as Paige might have expected. There were flickers of light there, as if someone had set small lights throughout the place.

Paige knew that she ought to wait there for backup. She should wait for Christopher to arrive, and only then go in to deal with the killer. If she did that, though, then Antoinette Couchon would still be in danger. She would still be in there with the killer, and he would be free to do what he wanted with her.

No, Paige had to go in now. She had to deal with this.

She got out of the car, readying her Glock and taking out a flashlight to shine beneath it. She left the shotgun in the trunk because, if there was a civilian there with the killer who might find herself used as a human shield, Paige didn't want a weapon that might potentially hit them both.

Not that she wanted to have to shoot anyone. Paige wanted to get in there, make the arrest, and make sure that this killer never had a chance to hurt anyone again.

She slipped into the park, ducking under a chain set across the path. There were more chains set at intervals, in a chaotic spider's web that lent an eerie air to the whole place.

Lanterns had been set in the trees, the light from them reflecting from the chains across the paths. Paige had to duck under those chains, pausing each time to make sure that there was no one waiting to ambush her. In the dark, it would have been easy for the killer to hide, ready to spring out on Paige as she approached.

Did he know that she was coming? Paige didn't think so. She hadn't announced her arrival, and she was trying to move as quietly as she could, but she still couldn't shake the feeling of eyes on her as she made her way through the park.

Paige's flashlight picked out the branches around her, reaching out like dark tendrils against the light. Paige had to brush branches aside to make any progress, pushing through the overgrown foliage of the park, trying to watch out for any danger ahead.

It was too close to the way things had been back when Paige had been fourteen, looking for her father out in the woods. Back then, she'd been as determined as she was now. She'd been sure that she would be the one to find him, because she was the one who'd spent plenty of time in the woods with him. She was the one who had known every inch of those woods.

She was the one who had found her father.

For several seconds, all she could do was stand there, paralyzed by the memory. Paige stood there, stuck with the image of her father dead on the ground in front of her. He'd been sprawled against a tree, held in place by ropes, utterly pale and empty of blood.

Paige could still remember the terror she'd felt in that moment, and the horror. She hadn't been able to move, hadn't been able to think. She'd only been able to stand there, and stare, and eventually scream so loud that people had come running. People had found her, standing there over her father's body. They had come and taken her away, asked her questions, tried to help.

The pain of that moment was still as fresh as it had been on the day Paige had found her father. It was still enough that she could barely move with it, that her breath came in quick pants that didn't seem to take in enough oxygen. She could only stand with her back pressed against a tree, the solidity of it the only thing holding her upright right then.

Paige forced herself to take deep breaths. She couldn't let herself be stopped by her memories, however traumatic they were. She *wasn't* that little girl anymore. She was a fully trained federal agent, and there was a civilian in danger from a serial killer. Paige had to act now. She had to do something to intervene.

Paige slowly managed to move away from the tree, putting one foot in front of the other, taking deep breaths as she went. This wasn't about her; this was about catching a killer.

Paige guessed that the space that had been used for performances was at the center of the park, but actually finding her way to it was harder than she expected. The whole place couldn't be that large, because in Las Vegas, a huge, unused space would quickly find itself redeveloped. Yet the whole place was so tangled, the trails so broken up by the chains, that it was almost impossible not to get turned around.

Then Paige heard the screams somewhere ahead, and suddenly she knew which direction she needed to go in.

"Help! Somebody help me!"

"That's it!" a man's voice said. "Play it up for the audience. Let them really hear how scared you are, Antoinette!"

Paige hurried towards the sounds, weaving her way through the pathways, not caring now about the branches that whipped past her face. The lanterns still hung in the branches, and Paige followed them as much as the screams.

"Help!"

Paige ran forward, still trying to watch for danger, but knowing that she didn't have much time left now. This killer had picked methods that used asphyxiation for some of his victims, but that didn't mean he would do things the same way now. The magic trick was the important part for him, and there were plenty of those that might involve shooting or stabbing. Any moment Paige wasted might be the one in which Antoinette Couchon died.

She came out into a large, open space covered in grass that had grown to knee height. There were folding chairs set out in that space, as if in anticipation of an audience. Those chairs looked new, as if they'd only just been put there recently.

They were arranged in rows in front of a broad stage. That stage was anything but new. It looked as if it had been there fifty years or more. It was painted in a mixture of white, blue, and gold, but those colors were faded and the paint was peeling. There were spots where the wood was rotten, and a couple of planks had given way completely.

Posters had been put up around the stage, each proclaiming a different magician from the past. There was Chung Ling Soo, Harry Houdini, and there among them, the Great Supremus.

The stage was set for a magic show. There were mechanisms set up there, including a couple of empty door frames, a rope that seemed to be hanging up with no support, a large set of blades sticking into a box from all angles, and…

And in the middle of it all, a box was sitting atop trestle stands. It was brightly, almost gaudily painted in red and cream, as if to suggest blood spraying from skin.

A woman was trapped in that box. She was probably in her fifties, blonde haired and with a beauty mark that Paige could make out even from a distance. She looked terrified, and was thrashing against the confines of the box that held her.

"Help me!" she pleaded. "He's coming back. Please, help me!"

Paige wanted to rush forward to free her, but she could also remember her training. That training said to make sure that the area was safe before moving to help victims, because otherwise, there was a risk of being turned into just one more person who needed to be saved.

It meant that Paige had to advance on the stage slowly, weapon raised, looking out for any sign of the killer. Had he just abandoned his victim? No, Paige couldn't believe that. This was the victim who meant the most to him, the one for whom the others had been just copies or practice runs for this moment.

No, Antoinette was right: the killer would be coming back. Paige needed to see him coming. She needed to be ready, because she had no doubt now that he was planning to ambush her, and then finish the murder. She advanced on the stage, pace by pace, trying to cover all of the angles.

There was a flash and a burst of smoke on the stage, and Paige ran towards it, ready to fire. A figure stepped from that smoke, dressed in a dress suit, top hat, and mask. He was carrying a saw, its wickedly sharp teeth glinting under the lights of the stage.

"Stephen Booth, freeze!" Paige called out. She wanted him to know that she knew who he was. She wanted him to know that even if he escaped they would catch him.

He took off his mask then, tossing it aside to reveal a remarkably handsome face beneath. Was he giving in?

"I guess if you know who I am, I don't need the mask," he said. "Who are you?"

"I'm Agent King, with the FBI," Paige said. "Put the saw down, put your hands behind your head, and get down on your knees."

"With the FBI?" Stephen said. "Ah, my audience. I hope you appreciated my efforts with my other effects. Putting a new spin on such classic tricks took some work."

He was moving towards the helpless form of Antoinette as he talked. Slowly, but he *was* moving.

"Is that what you call murdering three women?" Paige demanded. "Stand still, or I *will* shoot you."

"What, before my big finale?" Stephen said. "Did you like my effort with the shark tank, Agent King? I got the idea from your work."

He kept moving towards Antoinette, and that meant that Paige had a decision to make. She knew that she ought to shoot him. A serial killer was advancing on a woman he wanted to kill, with a weapon in his hand. Her trainers would have told her not to hesitate.

But Paige knew what it was like to shoot someone. She'd done it with Adam Riker. She wanted to give Stephen Booth every chance to surrender before she pulled the trigger.

Paige fired a warning shot instead, aimed at one of the lights on the stage. Paige had been good with her weapon on the range, and the light blew out with a pop.

"This is your last warning," Paige said as she kept advancing on the stage. "Put the weapon down!"

Stephen started to raise his hands. "You don't know what this woman did. You don't know the way she tormented me, and helped my father to torment me."

"Give yourself up, and we can talk about it," Paige said. She climbed the steps to the stage, closing in on him.

"No," Stephen said. "I don't think I will."

He flung his hands in Paige's direction, and doves burst from his sleeves. They flew at Paige's face, which meant that as she fired on Stephen, she missed. He ran for the box, and Paige knew that if she let him get there, Antoinette Couchon was going to die.

CHAPTER TWENTY EIGHT

Paige rushed for Stephen, but he was already ducking behind the box that held Antoinette, using her as a human shield. Paige kept her distance then because Stephen was still armed. If she rushed around the box to grab him, then she might find herself running into a saw coming the other way.

She worked to get an angle instead, gun held out ready to use. At this point, Paige was ready to fire. Stephen Booth was leaving her with no other choice now. She could see him trying to work the saw into position in a groove in the box.

"The show must go on!" he called out.

"Stephen, you need to give this up," Paige said. She was still working to get an angle, but he was rotating with her, making it hard to see enough of him to get a clean shot.

"A show needs its grand climax," the killer replied. "A build to the finish, followed by rapturous applause from the audience!"

"What audience?" Paige asked. The seats out in front of the stage were completely empty. "Do you think anyone cares about what you're doing?"

If he was doing this for the attention, then maybe that would be enough to taunt him into showing himself. Maybe Paige would be able to end this and save the woman who would otherwise be his last victim.

"There's no reason for you to do this, Stephen!" Antoinette said.

"There's *every* reason. If you hadn't been there, if it had just been me and my father, things would have been different. You made my life hell, then you took the inheritance that should have been mine."

Stephen started to work the saw back and forth, obviously determined to find a way to kill Antoinette even with Paige closing in on him. She heard Antoinette scream, and Paige knew in that moment that there was no time in which to look for the perfect shot anymore. She had to move in and stop this, or the woman was going to die.

Paige rushed forward, heading for the spot where Stephen was hiding. He reared up as Paige did so, swinging the saw he held at Paige as if he might try to cut her in half. Paige barely dodged back in time, her shot going wide as she did it.

Stephen took another swing at her, and Paige managed to step inside the swing, getting a grip on Stephen's forearm with her free hand while she tried to bring her gun to bear. He grabbed her wrist, though, the two of them standing inches from each other, struggling with all their might.

The problem was that Stephen was bigger than her, and obviously stronger. Paige felt him slowly turning her gun away from him, wrenching her arm hard enough that the Glock fell from her fingers, clattering to the floor of the stage. Stephen took hold of his saw with both hands, and now his strength meant that it descended slowly towards Paige's throat.

Paige snapped her head forward, slamming her forehead into the bridge of Stephen Booth's nose. He staggered back, and Paige lunged for her gun, managing to get her hand to it. She spun towards Stephen, but he kicked her, his foot cracking into Paige's skull. She managed to keep her grip on the weapon, but even so went spinning to the floor of the stage.

Paige rolled to her back, raising the weapon. If Stephen had been rearing over her, Paige would have fired then without hesitation, knowing that it was the only way to save her own life.

He hadn't advanced on her, though. Instead, he was making another lunge for the box.

"Stop!" Paige called out, her head still swimming with the impact of the kick she'd taken. The world around her seemed blurry, so that two Stephens advanced on the helpless form of Antoinette.

Paige fired again, and saw Stephen jerk back, but he didn't fall. He'd been grazed at best. Paige had missed again, unable to focus on her target enough to hit him. She could barely concentrate; she'd been hit that hard. She felt sick, felt like just curling up and giving in, but Paige forced herself to her knees, and then to her feet.

She heard Stephen curse, and then run back from the box that held Antoinette. Paige tried to focus, tried to get a clean shot, but her head was swimming so much that it felt almost impossible. She saw Stephen walk back towards one of the door frames set there on the stage, and Paige forced herself into a shooting stance, the way she'd been taught in the academy. This time, she wouldn't miss.

There was a flash, and for a second or two, it appeared that Stephen was standing in middle of the other doorway on the stage, having suddenly gone from one to the other like it was nothing. It meant that

Paige had to try to readjust her aim, taking a second or two to get back on target while her head still swam with dizziness.

There was another burst of smoke then, filling the doorway even as Paige tried to fire. She didn't see her bullet hit anything. Instead, the smoke cleared, and suddenly the doorway was empty. Stephen was gone, vanished as if he had genuinely teleported out of there.

Paige had no idea where he'd gone. A part of her simply didn't have any idea what was going on with the magic trick, and another part of her was still trying to get her head straight after being kicked. That one felt as if it had concussed her badly, leaving Paige to stagger over to the box that held Antoinette, struggling to open it.

There were catches on the side, and each one had been fastened in place by a simple metal pin, designed to allow the magician to let an assistant out quickly. It also meant that there was no way for Antoinette to let herself out from the inside. Paige pulled those pins out of the way, letting her open the box to help pull Antoinette from it.

The former magician's assistant had a long, ragged cut across her stomach, but it seemed shallow, and wasn't bleeding heavily. Paige helped her to her feet.

"Oh God, he was going to kill me," Antoinette said. She sounded as though she was panicking. "He cut me! I'm bleeding!"

Paige knew that she had to try to calm Antoinette down. Panicking would only make things worse, making her go into shock faster and making it harder for Paige to get her out of there safely. She needed to get Antoinette to focus on something else.

"Do you have any idea where he went?" Paige asked. "How does that effect work?"

"There are a couple of versions," Antoinette said. "But the one Henry always did involved a mechanism that triggered a trapdoor, letting him drop down beneath the stage. We always enjoyed doing it here because there are some old tunnels running underneath the park. It meant that we could do reappearances out in the audience, or up in one of the trees in the park."

Paige went over to the door frame that Stephen had vanished from, but then she saw the mirror there near the door.

She remembered the mirror on stage for Clarissa Bale's murder. What had Christopher called it? Pepper's Ghost? He'd projected his image into this doorway. It was the other one that mattered.

Paige went over to the other doorway. There, she heard footsteps down beneath the stage, along with panting that sounded as though

Stephen Booth was in pain. Had Paige winged him with one of her shots?

Even if she had, she knew that wasn't enough. He was still in a position where he might escape, especially if what Antoinette said about the tunnels was true. She had to get after him and bring him to justice. And if her shot had done more than just graze him, he might be in need of medical attention to ensure that he could be brought in alive to stand trial.

Paige knew that she had to go after him, but she also didn't like the idea of simply abandoning Antoinette when the killer might still be about. For all Paige knew, he was waiting for the moment when Paige went after him in order to try to kill Antoinette once more.

Paige's phone rang while she was still considering that problem. She was relieved to see that it was Christopher calling. Paige took the call, hoping that he wasn't too far away.

"Paige, are you there? I'm on my way to the park," he said.

That was good to hear; Paige had wanted to do all of this alone to prove that she could, but now, she found herself wishing Christopher were there to back her up.

"I've found the killer," Paige said. "He tried to kill a final victim, but I stopped him. He's currently trying to escape."

"I'm two minutes out," Christopher said. "Don't do anything before I arrive, Paige."

"Hurry," Paige replied, and hung up.

Don't do anything? She knew it was the right advice. She ought to just wait for Christopher, but the problem with that was the very real risk that the killer might get away.

Especially if Antoinette was right about the tunnels down there below the park. Those meant that Stephen had a ready-made escape route. Maybe that was the whole reason he'd chosen this spot for this "performance," reasoning that he had a way to get out of there without being caught if anything went wrong.

If so, Paige wasn't sure that she could wait for Christopher even now. She had to get after Stephen, or risk losing him completely.

"How does the mechanism work?" Paige asked Antoinette, taking her to the frame. "How do you activate it?"

"There's a catch here," Antoinette said, pointing it out. Until she showed it to Paige, Paige couldn't see it. It was practically invisible against the frame.

Paige stood within that frame. "So I just stand here and press it?"

"Yes, but… you're going to leave me here?"

"My partner is going to be here in a minute. I can't let Stephen get away."

Paige stood within that frame, holstering her gun so that it wouldn't go off as she fell. She took a deep breath, and then hit the button.

The floor fell away from under her feet, at for a moment, Paige tumbled down into emptiness. She kept her arms in, not wanting to hit the trapdoor on the way down. It only took her a second or two to fall, but there was still that feeling of weightlessness there, that feeling of hanging in space.

She hit a large crash mat that had obviously been placed there for just that purpose. Paige felt the impact of the fall, and rolled to her feet, getting out her gun again and looking around to try to find Stephen.

The saw he'd been using lay abandoned on the ground, along with several boxes of what looked like props. There was a barrel full of oversized swords that were clearly designed to be as showy as possible on stage, and a couple of boxes of scarves and rings, balls, and giant cards, as if Stephen hadn't been sure what to bring out on stage.

Paige could hear footsteps now, beyond the room she was in. There was a doorway leading to what looked like a long tunnel, and Paige set off in that direction, a flashlight held under her gun, following the sound of the footsteps.

She found the source of the footsteps quickly enough. A phone sat on the ground, the sound coming from it with almost metronomic monotony. Paige felt a flash of fear then as she realized that she had been tricked.

She turned quickly, wanting to cover the way she'd come, and saw Stephen bearing down on her, a huge prop scimitar held ready to swing straight for her head.

CHAPTER TWENTY NINE

Paige ducked on instinct, the sword passing right through the space where her neck had been. The weight of it took it around into the wall beside Paige, striking sparks from it and gouging a line into it that suggested that the blade was more than sharp enough that it could take her head off.

In the confines of the tunnel, only Paige's small size saved her, because it meant that she was able to roll past Stephen, back towards the room in which she'd just landed. She tried to turn and bring up the gun she held, but Stephen was swinging that huge sword again, and this time it smashed into the Glock, sending it skittering away into the darkness of the tunnel.

"You had to interfere!" Stephen said, his fury twisting his otherwise handsome features. "You couldn't just let me finish my act!"

"It's not an act, Stephen. People are dying."

"People die!" he shot back. "So what? Antoinette deserves it!"

"And did the others?" Paige backed away slowly, working her way into the room where she'd first landed. It gave her some more room to try to dodge that huge blade.

"They were just like her!" Stephen roared. "Do you think I couldn't see it written on their faces?"

"They all had beauty marks, that's all." Paige was doing her best to reason with him or, failing that, to simply stall for long enough that she could think of something else. The last thing she wanted to do was try to take on a man with a sword with nothing but her bare hands.

"And when I saw them, I knew that they deserved to die," Stephen said. "The same way you do. The cut and restored federal agent."

Paige assumed that was some kind of reference to a magic trick, but she had no time to think about it, because Stephen was already swinging for her again. Paige threw herself backwards, tripped over the crash mat that had broken her fall, and barely rolled up onto her feet again before the killer brought the prop scimitar down in a two handed sweep aimed at the spot where she'd been lying.

Sheer terror propelled Paige into movement. She might have trained to bring down suspects, but nothing in her training had included men with swords trying to cut her down. All Paige could do was improvise, and hope that she found a way.

Paige grabbed that mat, hauling it up between the two of them, trying to use it as an oversized shield as Stephen swung again. Its sheer bulk slowed down the blow, giving Paige a chance to kick the mat over into him. The mat tangled Stephen for a moment or two, giving Paige a chance to grab another of the prop swords from the barrel of them down there and bring it up in front of her.

"Just put the weapon down, Stephen," she said. "It's over. The FBI knows who you are now. Even if you get away, even if you somehow kill me, we'll hunt you down. There will be nowhere you can run that you won't be found."

"I'm good at disappearing," Stephen assured her, and took another swing at Paige with the sword.

Paige's FBI training hadn't covered sword fighting, but it *had* covered hand to hand combat and the use of weapons. Meanwhile, she got the feeling that Stephen didn't actually know what he was doing with the prop sword he held. Instead, he whirled it and swung it like he was showing off for an audience.

The only problem was that he had enough of an advantage in size and strength that it almost didn't matter. When Paige parried his first blow, the sheer force of it made her take a step back. She ducked under another, swinging back at him as best she could. Paige didn't want to close the distance on him, though, not when he might be able to overpower her.

Stephen parried Paige's blow, then swung back, forcing her to block again. The two of them traded sword strokes for several seconds, neither of them truly knowing what they were doing. Paige had trained with a baton when she was learning to be an agent, but a sword wasn't a baton, especially not some oversized one like this.

The only part that mattered was the one thing her instructors had drilled into her: in any fight, she had to be aggressive. She had to try to overwhelm the suspect quickly, and end the fight before they had a chance to kill her or hurt civilians.

Paige swung the sword quickly, making multiple swift attacks that tried to probe Stephen's defenses. She struck and struck, keeping him on the back foot, trying not to give him a chance to make attacks. If she could keep him parrying and moving back, then maybe an opportunity would open up for Paige to trip him, or even to thrust the prop sword home.

Paige saw an opening, and knew that she should take it, but in that moment she found herself hesitating. She couldn't bring herself to simply kill someone. She wasn't a killer. Even with Adam Riker, the serial killer who had tormented her and gone after her mother, she had only wounded him. Paige held back now, and that hesitation cost her.

She saw Stephen pull a deck of cards from his pocket, but there was no time to react as he sprayed them out into her face in a cascade of cards. It made Paige stumble back, and in that moment, Stephen struck the sword from her hands, the sheer impact of his blow too great for her to hold onto it.

It clattered to the floor, and Paige had no time in which to reach for it, because Stephen was already winding up for another blow, aimed at her head again. There was no time to dodge sideways or back, so all Paige could do was duck down, letting another stroke of the sword pass over her head.

She didn't have any choice other than to work in close now, grabbing onto Stephen Booth's wrists with both hands as he raised the sword again, straightening her arms to keep him from forcing it down into her flesh. She kicked and kneed him, trying to get him to let go of the weapon, but there was a fury in his eyes that said he just didn't feel the pain.

He struck her then, sending Paige sprawling onto her back, looking up at the trapdoor above.

A moment later, Stephen Booth was in that space, standing above Paige with the sword raised, ready to kill her. He started to lower it towards her, and Paige reached up, grabbing for his wrists again, using all her strength to try to keep him off her.

It wasn't enough. Paige was putting every ounce of strength she had into trying to keep Stephen away from her, but his weight and his strength were greater. The sword inched down towards her, and Paige knew that when it reached her throat, he would just keep pushing it all the way through her flesh. He would kill her and then he would go back to try to kill Antoinette again.

Paige struggled, trying to create some space, trying to break free, but it didn't make any difference. The blade kept descending towards her throat, and Paige was certain that she was going to die.

Then Paige saw Christopher standing above, visible through the trapdoor, lit by the lights of the stage above. He stood there, staring down at what was going on, his weapon out and leveled, like he was looking for a clear shot.

Yet with Paige and Stephen so close, there was no way that he would get one. Bullets traveled. It was one of the first things that they taught on the firing range at the academy. Shoot a bad guy, and that bullet could easily pass through to hit an innocent civilian beyond. In this case, Christopher might kill her even as he tried to save her.

He seemed to realize that, and then he did something that Paige really didn't expect. He dropped through the trapdoor feet first.

He slammed into Stephen's back, making him cry out and sending him sprawling. The sword went tumbling from his hand.

Paige was on her feet in an instant, trying to get after him and bring him down to the ground. Even stunned by the impact of Christopher's entrance, though, he was still fast enough to avoid Paige's attempt to grab him.

He ran for the tunnel and Paige set off after him. There were twists and turns down here, and Paige did her best to follow him, not wanting to let him get too far ahead. A couple of turnings, though, and he was quickly out of sight.

Paige heard the sound of his running footsteps ahead.

She followed the sound, snatching up her gun again as she passed the spot where she'd dropped it. She guessed that she should be grateful that Stephen hadn't spotted it to pick it up.

"You could have waited for me," Christopher said as the two of them padded forward, advancing on the sound of the footsteps.

"He was getting away."

"I meant before that," Christopher said. "You should have waited for me before heading into the park."

"There was imminent danger to the next victim," Paige replied. She saw Christopher look over at her with surprise, but then nod.

The two of them kept heading through the tunnels beneath the park, following the sound of the footsteps. They were closing in now. The footsteps were closer.

Only Paige remembered what had happened *last* time she'd closed in on that sound. She and Christopher kept moving towards it, rounding a corner in the dark, their flashlights the only glimmer of light there. The footsteps were very close now.

Paige saw the phone there on the ground, and she was already turning, dropping to one knee as she did so.

Stephen Booth was coming up behind them, another blade in his hand. This one was short and utilitarian, but it would still kill them as quickly. As soon as he saw Paige turning, Stephen sprinted for her, the blade raised.

In that moment, she was back in the forest where Adam Riker had tried to kill her mother. She was back standing over her father's corpse. She was at every crime scene she'd been to, staring at every corpse she'd seen so far. In that moment, it would have been so easy to be overwhelmed by the horror of all of it, so easy to simply freeze in the face of the killer rushing her.

Paige didn't freeze.

Instead, Paige fired once, the bullet slamming into the shoulder of the serial killer's raised weapon arm. Stephen went down, screaming and clutching his shoulder, in obvious agony as he fell.

"A good magician never repeats the same trick twice," she said, as she went over to him.

Her heart was pounding, the terror of the last few seconds finally hitting her. Still, Paige did the things that she knew she was meant to do. She kicked the knife away, making sure that Stephen wouldn't be able to use it again. She covered him, while Christopher moved in, wrenching his arms behind his back and cuffing him.

"Stephen Booth, you're under arrest."

CHAPTER THIRTY

It was an awkward flight back to Washington. Paige and Christopher had solved the case, but Paige still wasn't sure about the way that things stood between the two of them. Could she really work with someone when things were so difficult? When she spent every moment with him having to be careful not to go too far, not to say or do the wrong thing?

Even being stuffed into an airplane seat next to him was difficult, because it meant that Paige had to spend the whole flight back to D.C. just inches from him, closer than she'd allowed herself to be in all the time she'd been in Las Vegas.

Being that close, it was hard not to reach out to touch him, no matter how much she knew that she couldn't. Paige had to tell herself again that her feelings didn't matter. That she and Christopher could only be partners. That they *had* to be partners because this was the only job where Paige could find out what she needed to know about her father's killer.

Paige knew all of that, but it didn't make being this close to Christopher without being able to do anything any easier.

"Are you sure that one of us shouldn't stay to make sure that everything goes smoothly?" Paige asked.

"The plane's in the air now," Christopher pointed out. "Besides, you caught Stephen Booth red handed trying to kill Antoinette Couchon. Once he gets out of the hospital, he'll confess, and even if he doesn't, there's more than enough to get a conviction."

Christopher sounded pleased.

"You… did well, Paige."

There was a hesitation there that Paige couldn't quite read, as if Christopher were worried about complimenting her like that.

"You did your part too," Paige pointed out.

"Yes, we make a good team."

Christopher sounded almost regretful about that, as if he would rather they didn't work together quite so well. Maybe he'd been hoping for an excuse to swap Paige out for a new partner. He might not be able to guess the reasons that Paige was making things so awkward between them, but he could probably sense that there *was* that awkwardness. Anyone sensible would want to run from it, to find a partner he actually had some chemistry with.

Of course, the problem for Paige was too *much* chemistry, rather than too little.

"You saved my life back there, in the space under the stage," Paige said.

"That's what partners are for," Christopher replied.

"No, Christopher, I mean it. If you hadn't been there, I would have died."

"So maybe next time, don't go running off without me," Christopher suggested.

Next time. That was the thing now: they were partners, working on the same team. There would be more serial killers for the two of them to face, more victims to find answers for. In order for that to happen, Paige would need to find a way to work with Christopher without the attraction she felt every time she looked his way causing a problem.

She just hoped that she would be able to do that.

"I won't have to run off if you listen to me next time," Paige pointed out. "Did you ever find out why Mark Zint wasn't talking?"

"Detective Sanchez texted me. It turns out that there were more women he'd been harassing, and he was worried about it coming out. At the time of Sienna Niven's murder, he was off sleeping with a fan."

That explained that part of it, at least.

"Detective Sanchez is going to be happy to see the back of us," Paige ventured, struggling to try to find a safe topic of conversation. She glanced over to Christopher, saw him staring back at her, and glanced away again.

"I think she's happy enough that she's been involved in the successful hunt for a murderer," Christopher said. He paused, not saying anything for several seconds. "Look, Paige…"

What was he going to say? That question sent a thrill of worry running through Paige. Was he going to tell her that he'd noticed how awkward things were between them and guessed the cause? Was he going to tell her that they needed to keep things strictly professional, and that if she couldn't do that, she was going to have to find a new partner?

It wasn't like those were things she didn't already know.

"Yes?" Paige said.

Christopher shook his head, though. "Nothing. I just wanted to say that we make a good team. When we get back to Quantico, I'll let Sauer know that you were the one who found the crucial breakthrough in this case. He should know that you're more than capable of pulling your weight as an agent."

That praise both sent pride swelling through Paige and hurt more than she could say. She was proud, because Christopher was the one person from whom praise of that kind truly mattered. He'd been the one to pick her out to work with him in the first place, the one who had insisted that her insights into killers might be enough to let the two of them catch them.

At the same time, it hurt because it was a long way short of everything Paige wanted to hear from Christopher. There was a layer of reservation to it all that felt faint and cold and professional. It was short even of what Paige would have hoped for from a partner, let alone a friend, or…

Or nothing. Christopher was her partner, that was all.

Honestly, Paige wasn't sure about what to do when it came to the situation with Christopher. The attraction she'd felt since the moment she met him felt as though it was tearing her apart, yet she couldn't put distance between the two of them, because she needed to work at the BAU. She needed to be there in the department Christopher worked in or she wouldn't be able to get close to finding her father's killer.

That mattered to Paige more than anything. She didn't pull up her personal files on the case, not here on the flight, not where Christopher could see them, but that didn't matter. Paige had most of them memorized by this point anyway. She went over the facts in her head, again and again.

She needed more, and hopefully, now that she had shown her worth with this case, she would *get* more. Agent Sauer had said that she could have details of the Exsanguination Killer's most recent murders once she was done with this case. Paige had done her part. It was time for her new boss to make good on his word.

*

Paige stood outside Agent Sauer's office in Quantico, determined to be patient while she waited for him to see her. He was currently in there with a couple of agents, having a discussion that looked incredibly serious.

It was only that discussion that stopped her from just bursting in there to demand the answers that he had promised her. Well, that and the fact that she wanted to keep her job. She needed to keep her job, because that was the only way Paige was going to stay in a position to potentially catch the man who had killed her father.

Paige didn't go away, though, didn't go back to her desk to work on whatever was waiting for her next. Christopher was already back there, writing up his report for the case. Paige would need to do the same thing, but right now, she needed to talk to Agent Sauer. She needed answers on the Exsanguination Killer case, because she hadn't been able to sleep last night, wouldn't be able to sleep today without those answers.

By the time the two agents left, Paige was itching with the need to talk to her boss. Almost as soon as they were out of the door, Paige knocked and stepped inside Sauer's office.

The office was neat to an almost obsessive degree, every file aligned perfectly, the desk perfectly clean and minimalist. There were a couple of citations and pictures up on the walls, but even those were aligned with absolute precision.

"Agent King," he said. "Congratulations on solving your first case as an agent. Agent Marriott tells me that you were the one to make the link between the victims."

"Thank you, sir," Paige said.

"Although the Las Vegas PD did raise a couple of issues with me. Something about a civilian being pushed into a shark tank during an attempt to apprehend him, and a well-known figure being wrongly arrested."

"The first case was a suspect who slipped while trying to run from us, and who has now been arrested for helping people to cheat in the casino," Paige said. "With the second, we had plenty of good reasons to think that he might be a suspect."

"Just make sure you put those reasons in your report, in case there's anything more from the Las Vegas PD," Sauer said. He said it as if he expected Paige to run off then and start to work on her report immediately.

Maybe Paige should have, but her need to know more about her father's killer stopped her from doing it. Paige kept standing there in front of Sauer's desk instead, forcing herself to say the next words.

"Sir, you said that once this case was done, you would bring me up to speed on what's happening with the Exsanguination Killer."

Agent Sauer looked over his desk at her, blinking as he obviously tried to remember saying it. Paige caught the moment when he did remember, because there was a slight frown there on his face as he did so.

"Agent King, I know about your personal connection to this case. Are you sure you want to hear the details of it like this?"

Paige nodded without hesitation. "More than anything. I need to know the truth about what's going on. I need to know about the Exsanguination killer. I've pieced together some details, but I know there's a lot that the FBI hasn't released about the crimes."

"That's true," Agent Sauer said, and as he said it, he pushed a file across his desk from the very top of his pile. In spite of the moment he'd taken to think, it was obvious that he'd prepared for this moment. "Here's a copy for you to read, but I can give you most of the details now, if you'd prefer."

Paige nodded, although she got the feeling that Sauer would have told her all of this anyway. She suspected that he was watching her reactions, trying to see how she responded to the information about her father's killer.

"All right," Sauer said. "Why don't you start by telling me what *you* know, King?"

He was obviously trying to judge how deeply she'd gone into this already. Paige had the information at her fingertips, stored away in her memory through simple repetition.

"The Exsanguination Killer has been operating for at least eleven years," Paige said. "My father was his third victim, part of a sequence of three that he completed before he disappeared the first time. Approximately a year later, he killed another set of three people. That has been his pattern since: appearing, killing in threes. There is no obvious pattern to his victims. He has killed both men and women, although slightly more men."

Paige tried to deliver it like it was just simple information. Like her memories weren't trying to drag her back into the moment when she'd found her father. She played the part of a cool, professional agent, because she knew that was what was most likely to get her the information she needed.

"His methods have been consistent," Paige said.

"His?" Sauer said. "There has been some speculation that this killer might be a woman, given that the Exsanguination Killer targets so many men, and the methods don't rely on strength."

"I'm playing the odds, sir," Paige said. "Statistically, the majority of serial killers are male, and the few women tend to kill in different ways."

Sauer shrugged, as if he weren't convinced yet. "The methods?"

"The Exsanguination Killer immobilizes their victims with drugs and restraints, usually in outdoor areas," Paige said. "Then they open major veins in their victims, and leave them to bleed out. My guess is that they stay to watch that process."

"Why?" Sauer asked.

"Because why do something so slow otherwise?" Paige asked. "Or at least, why do something so slow that doesn't cause much pain? The victims aren't being left to die in agony alone. They're being watched while they die."

Sauer nodded. "It seems that you know quite a bit. All right. Now for the parts that don't get released to the public. The murder weapon appears to be a surgical scalpel, or some equally small, sharp blade. The killer makes cuts vertically along veins, making it harder to save victims even if they're found. And, in one of each set of victims, the killer leaves a note."

He opened the file he'd pushed to Paige, letting her see a photograph of a note.

You will not catch me. This is necessary. It must happen, and it will. You cannot stop me. You can only watch, as I watch.

The note was not signed, even with the nom de guerre given to the killer. Instead, blood had been dropped onto the page, and something had been pressed into it to make a design, almost the way someone might use a wax seal. The design was in the shape of a seahorse.

It was a detail that hadn't been released to the public, and so Paige didn't have it in her files at home. This was new. She just had to hope that it would be enough to lead her to him.

So that she could kill him.

NOW AVAILABLE!

THE GIRL HE WISHED
(A Paige King FBI Suspense Thriller—Book 4)

Paige King, a Ph.D. in forensic psychology and a new arrival at the FBI's elite BAU unit, has an uncanny ability to enter serial killers' minds. But when a new serial killer strikes, leaving a cryptic signature of a fleur de lis at each crime scene, Paige wonders: will this diabolical killer outsmart them all?

"A masterpiece of thriller and mystery."
—Books and Movie Reviews, Roberto Mattos (re *Once Gone*)

THE GIRL HE WISHED is book #4 in a new series by #1 bestselling and critically acclaimed mystery and suspense author Blake Pierce.

A complex psychological crime thriller full of twists and turns and packed with heart-pounding suspense, the PAIGE KING mystery series will make you fall in love with a brilliant new female protagonist and keep you turning pages late into the night. It is a perfect addition for fans of Rachel Caine, Teresa Driscoll and Robert Dugoni.

Books #5 and #6 in the series—THE GIRL HE CROWNED and THE GIRL HE WATCHED—are now also available!

"An edge of your seat thriller in a new series that keeps you turning pages! ...So many twists, turns and red herrings... I can't wait to see what happens next."
—Reader review (*Her Last Wish*)

"A strong, complex story about two FBI agents trying to stop a serial killer. If you want an author to capture your attention and have you guessing, yet trying to put the pieces together, Pierce is your author!"
—Reader review (*Her Last Wish*)

"A typical Blake Pierce twisting, turning, roller coaster ride suspense thriller. Will have you turning the pages to the last sentence of the last chapter!!!"
—Reader review (*City of Prey*)

"Right from the start we have an unusual protagonist that I haven't seen done in this genre before. The action is nonstop… A very atmospheric novel that will keep you turning pages well into the wee hours."
—Reader review (*City of Prey*)

"Everything that I look for in a book… a great plot, interesting characters, and grabs your interest right away. The book moves along at a breakneck pace and stays that way until the end. Now on go I to book two!"
—Reader review (*Girl, Alone*)

"Exciting, heart pounding, edge of your seat book… a must read for mystery and suspense readers!"
—Reader review (*Girl, Alone*)

Blake Pierce

Blake Pierce is the USA Today bestselling author of the RILEY PAGE mystery series, which includes seventeen books. Blake Pierce is also the author of the MACKENZIE WHITE mystery series, comprising fourteen books; of the AVERY BLACK mystery series, comprising six books; of the KERI LOCKE mystery series, comprising five books; of the MAKING OF RILEY PAIGE mystery series, comprising six books; of the KATE WISE mystery series, comprising seven books; of the CHLOE FINE psychological suspense mystery, comprising six books; of the JESSE HUNT psychological suspense thriller series, comprising twenty four books; of the AU PAIR psychological suspense thriller series, comprising three books; of the ZOE PRIME mystery series, comprising six books; of the ADELE SHARP mystery series, comprising fifteen books, of the EUROPEAN VOYAGE cozy mystery series, comprising four books; of the new LAURA FROST FBI suspense thriller, comprising nine books (and counting); of the new ELLA DARK FBI suspense thriller, comprising eleven books (and counting); of the A YEAR IN EUROPE cozy mystery series, comprising nine books, of the AVA GOLD mystery series, comprising six books (and counting); of the RACHEL GIFT mystery series, comprising eight books (and counting); of the VALERIE LAW mystery series, comprising nine books (and counting); of the PAIGE KING mystery series, comprising six books (and counting); of the MAY MOORE mystery series, comprising six books (and counting); and the CORA SHIELDS mystery series, comprising three books (and counting).

An avid reader and lifelong fan of the mystery and thriller genres, Blake loves to hear from you, so please feel free to visit www.blakepierceauthor.com to learn more and stay in touch.

BOOKS BY BLAKE PIERCE

CORA SHIELDS MYSTERY SERIES
UNDONE (Book #1)
UNWANTED (Book #2)
UNHINGED (Book #3)

MAY MOORE SUSPENSE THRILLER
NEVER RUN (Book #1)
NEVER TELL (Book #2)
NEVER LIVE (Book #3)
NEVER HIDE (Book #4)
NEVER FORGIVE (Book #5)
NEVER AGAIN (Book #6)

PAIGE KING MYSTERY SERIES
THE GIRL HE PINED (Book #1)
THE GIRL HE CHOSE (Book #2)
THE GIRL HE TOOK (Book #3)
THE GIRL HE WISHED (Book #4)
THE GIRL HE CROWNED (Book #5)
THE GIRL HE WATCHED (Book #6)

VALERIE LAW MYSTERY SERIES
NO MERCY (Book #1)
NO PITY (Book #2)
NO FEAR (Book #3)
NO SLEEP (Book #4)
NO QUARTER (Book #5)
NO CHANCE (Book #6)
NO REFUGE (Book #7)
NO GRACE (Book #8)
NO ESCAPE (Book #9)

RACHEL GIFT MYSTERY SERIES
HER LAST WISH (Book #1)

HER LAST CHANCE (Book #2)
HER LAST HOPE (Book #3)
HER LAST FEAR (Book #4)
HER LAST CHOICE (Book #5)
HER LAST BREATH (Book #6)
HER LAST MISTAKE (Book #7)
HER LAST DESIRE (Book #8)

AVA GOLD MYSTERY SERIES
CITY OF PREY (Book #1)
CITY OF FEAR (Book #2)
CITY OF BONES (Book #3)
CITY OF GHOSTS (Book #4)
CITY OF DEATH (Book #5)
CITY OF VICE (Book #6)

A YEAR IN EUROPE
A MURDER IN PARIS (Book #1)
DEATH IN FLORENCE (Book #2)
VENGEANCE IN VIENNA (Book #3)
A FATALITY IN SPAIN (Book #4)

ELLA DARK FBI SUSPENSE THRILLER
GIRL, ALONE (Book #1)
GIRL, TAKEN (Book #2)
GIRL, HUNTED (Book #3)
GIRL, SILENCED (Book #4)
GIRL, VANISHED (Book 5)
GIRL ERASED (Book #6)
GIRL, FORSAKEN (Book #7)
GIRL, TRAPPED (Book #8)
GIRL, EXPENDABLE (Book #9)
GIRL, ESCAPED (Book #10)
GIRL, HIS (Book #11)

LAURA FROST FBI SUSPENSE THRILLER
ALREADY GONE (Book #1)
ALREADY SEEN (Book #2)
ALREADY TRAPPED (Book #3)

ALREADY MISSING (Book #4)
ALREADY DEAD (Book #5)
ALREADY TAKEN (Book #6)
ALREADY CHOSEN (Book #7)
ALREADY LOST (Book #8)
ALREADY HIS (Book #9)

EUROPEAN VOYAGE COZY MYSTERY SERIES
MURDER (AND BAKLAVA) (Book #1)
DEATH (AND APPLE STRUDEL) (Book #2)
CRIME (AND LAGER) (Book #3)
MISFORTUNE (AND GOUDA) (Book #4)
CALAMITY (AND A DANISH) (Book #5)
MAYHEM (AND HERRING) (Book #6)

ADELE SHARP MYSTERY SERIES
LEFT TO DIE (Book #1)
LEFT TO RUN (Book #2)
LEFT TO HIDE (Book #3)
LEFT TO KILL (Book #4)
LEFT TO MURDER (Book #5)
LEFT TO ENVY (Book #6)
LEFT TO LAPSE (Book #7)
LEFT TO VANISH (Book #8)
LEFT TO HUNT (Book #9)
LEFT TO FEAR (Book #10)
LEFT TO PREY (Book #11)
LEFT TO LURE (Book #12)
LEFT TO CRAVE (Book #13)
LEFT TO LOATHE (Book #14)
LEFT TO HARM (Book #15)

THE AU PAIR SERIES
ALMOST GONE (Book#1)
ALMOST LOST (Book #2)
ALMOST DEAD (Book #3)

ZOE PRIME MYSTERY SERIES
FACE OF DEATH (Book#1)

FACE OF MURDER (Book #2)
FACE OF FEAR (Book #3)
FACE OF MADNESS (Book #4)
FACE OF FURY (Book #5)
FACE OF DARKNESS (Book #6)

A JESSIE HUNT PSYCHOLOGICAL SUSPENSE SERIES
THE PERFECT WIFE (Book #1)
THE PERFECT BLOCK (Book #2)
THE PERFECT HOUSE (Book #3)
THE PERFECT SMILE (Book #4)
THE PERFECT LIE (Book #5)
THE PERFECT LOOK (Book #6)
THE PERFECT AFFAIR (Book #7)
THE PERFECT ALIBI (Book #8)
THE PERFECT NEIGHBOR (Book #9)
THE PERFECT DISGUISE (Book #10)
THE PERFECT SECRET (Book #11)
THE PERFECT FAÇADE (Book #12)
THE PERFECT IMPRESSION (Book #13)
THE PERFECT DECEIT (Book #14)
THE PERFECT MISTRESS (Book #15)
THE PERFECT IMAGE (Book #16)
THE PERFECT VEIL (Book #17)
THE PERFECT INDISCRETION (Book #18)
THE PERFECT RUMOR (Book #19)
THE PERFECT COUPLE (Book #20)
THE PERFECT MURDER (Book #21)
THE PERFECT HUSBAND (Book #22)
THE PERFECT SCANDAL (Book #23)
THE PERFECT MASK (Book #24)

CHLOE FINE PSYCHOLOGICAL SUSPENSE SERIES
NEXT DOOR (Book #1)
A NEIGHBOR'S LIE (Book #2)
CUL DE SAC (Book #3)
SILENT NEIGHBOR (Book #4)
HOMECOMING (Book #5)

TINTED WINDOWS (Book #6)

KATE WISE MYSTERY SERIES
IF SHE KNEW (Book #1)
IF SHE SAW (Book #2)
IF SHE RAN (Book #3)
IF SHE HID (Book #4)
IF SHE FLED (Book #5)
IF SHE FEARED (Book #6)
IF SHE HEARD (Book #7)

THE MAKING OF RILEY PAIGE SERIES
WATCHING (Book #1)
WAITING (Book #2)
LURING (Book #3)
TAKING (Book #4)
STALKING (Book #5)
KILLING (Book #6)

RILEY PAIGE MYSTERY SERIES
ONCE GONE (Book #1)
ONCE TAKEN (Book #2)
ONCE CRAVED (Book #3)
ONCE LURED (Book #4)
ONCE HUNTED (Book #5)
ONCE PINED (Book #6)
ONCE FORSAKEN (Book #7)
ONCE COLD (Book #8)
ONCE STALKED (Book #9)
ONCE LOST (Book #10)
ONCE BURIED (Book #11)
ONCE BOUND (Book #12)
ONCE TRAPPED (Book #13)
ONCE DORMANT (Book #14)
ONCE SHUNNED (Book #15)
ONCE MISSED (Book #16)
ONCE CHOSEN (Book #17)

MACKENZIE WHITE MYSTERY SERIES

BEFORE HE KILLS (Book #1)
BEFORE HE SEES (Book #2)
BEFORE HE COVETS (Book #3)
BEFORE HE TAKES (Book #4)
BEFORE HE NEEDS (Book #5)
BEFORE HE FEELS (Book #6)
BEFORE HE SINS (Book #7)
BEFORE HE HUNTS (Book #8)
BEFORE HE PREYS (Book #9)
BEFORE HE LONGS (Book #10)
BEFORE HE LAPSES (Book #11)
BEFORE HE ENVIES (Book #12)
BEFORE HE STALKS (Book #13)
BEFORE HE HARMS (Book #14)

AVERY BLACK MYSTERY SERIES
CAUSE TO KILL (Book #1)
CAUSE TO RUN (Book #2)
CAUSE TO HIDE (Book #3)
CAUSE TO FEAR (Book #4)
CAUSE TO SAVE (Book #5)
CAUSE TO DREAD (Book #6)

KERI LOCKE MYSTERY SERIES
A TRACE OF DEATH (Book #1)
A TRACE OF MURDER (Book #2)
A TRACE OF VICE (Book #3)
A TRACE OF CRIME (Book #4)
A TRACE OF HOPE (Book #5)